DIGITAL GOD

Nikhilkumar Singh is a film-maker and communications consultant specializing in sustainable agriculture initiatives. He studied at the Nutan Vidya Mandir, Fort Songadh, Surat, and holds a Master's degree in Communication Studies from Maharaja Sayajirao University, Vadodara. He lives in Bengaluru, Muzaffarpur and Hyderabad (one place at a time) and can be contacted at my.digital.god@gmail.com.

AF669255

DIGITAL GOD

NIKHILKUMAR SINGH

HARPER
BLACK

First published in India in 2016 by Harper Black
An imprint of HarperCollins *Publishers*

Copyright © Nikhilkumar Singh 2016

P-ISBN: 978-93-5029-682-0
E-ISBN: 978-93-5029-693-6

2 4 6 8 10 9 7 5 3 1

Nikhilkumar Singh asserts the moral right
to be identified as the author of this work.

This is a work of fiction and all characters and incidents described in this book are the product of the author's imagination. Any resemblance to actual persons, living or dead, is entirely coincidental.

All rights reserved. No part of this publication may be reproduced, stored in a retrieval system, or transmitted, in any form or by any means, electronic, mechanical, photocopying, recording or otherwise, without the prior permission of the publishers.

HarperCollins *Publishers*
A-75, Sector 57, Noida, Uttar Pradesh 201301, India
1 London Bridge Street, London SE1 9GF, United Kingdom
Hazelton Lanes, 55 Avenue Road, Suite 2900, Toronto, Ontario M5R 3L2
and 1995 Markham Road, Scarborough, Ontario M1B 5M8, Canada
25 Ryde Road, Pymble, Sydney, NSW 2073, Australia
195 Broadway, New York, NY 10007, USA

Typeset in 11/14.5 Sabon at
Manipal Digital Systems, Manipal

Printed and bound at
Replika Press Pvt. Ltd.

In memory of my friend, T.N. Anuradha

ONE

4 December 2006
Mission: Eliminate Kamsa

A figure in a blue turban, only his bloodshot eyes visible, turned around to see his handiwork – the burning palace. He watched the spectacle from a distance, his eyes reflecting the fiery-red flames.

'March on, warrior.' The stony voice of his instructor echoed in his ears. 'Your next target is Kamsa's palace. You must gain control of the magical sword to challenge Kamsa.'

The man in the blue turban drew out his sword, ready to take on his new enemy. Gazing up, he saw the golden palace beyond its towering gate.

He entered the palace in no time, taking out enemies as he searched for the magical sword. But the central location of the courtyard and the branching halls gave him no clear indication of the sword's location.

The clock ticked away.

Out of the corner of his eye, he spotted a giant ape running away. Its sheer size was intimidating.

'Don't go by the size of your enemies,' the stony voice announced. 'Kill it before it can vanish into the shadows.'

Emboldened by the voice of his instructor, the man ran after the ape, down the corridor and into the half-open door of a room. In front of him stood the devil king, Kamsa.

The man in the blue turban was not yet prepared for his enemy's assault. Not without the magical sword.

He ran around the periphery of the room, swinging his sword in every direction, trying to protect himself.

But before the man could act, Kamsa's blade came hurtling towards him, piercing his chest. He tumbled on to the floor, powerless, as he watched his own blood oozing down his hand.

Death at the hands of Kamsa was imminent.

Every other time the man had died, he had been up and running in about thirty seconds. But this was his *third* death. There was no escaping the final death.

'Game over,' announced the female voice as the text on the computer screen flashed: *You lost!*

Hands still firmly on the keyboard, Rahul was stunned by his defeat. Looking around, he saw the real world. In front of him lay the computer monitor in an open box-like cubicle that was painted orange and purple. It was as if he had been born again in a different world.

Like many teenaged boys of Rezimental Street in Secunderabad, Rahul Kumar enjoyed playing video games at the MNR Cyber Café. He was no pushover gamer, but today was not his day.

Rahul pulled aside his headphones and glanced at the clock at the bottom right corner of his computer screen. *11.00 a.m.* 'What? Two hours!' he muttered, glancing at the wall clock to confirm. 'One hour fifty minutes. Shit, that's thirty rupees!'

On his way out, he searched for the girl he often saw in the cyber café. Secretly, he hoped to see her. Maybe talk to her. He spotted her in Cabin 14, her usual seat, the one that was closest to the cashier's counter.

The MNR Cyber Café housed twenty-three computer stations. But the place was much more than cubicles and computers. It had portable gaming consoles, the latest software with a fast Internet connection and comfortable desk chairs: a rare combination that induced people to spend a fair portion of their day in the virtual world.

The cyber café shop was set up by two enterprising college students in 2002. Initially, the co-founders rented out their personal computers with Internet access to the public. Driven by the popularity of the latest games and fast Internet access, the venture soon took off.

The place was used by all types now, from the young crowd to journalists searching for information to middle-aged executives posting their résumé. But mostly the place was filled with college students, who were the loyal patrons of the café.

The café manager of the day and part-owner, Bansi Bettary, was typing from a sheet of paper placed on the top of the logbook. His workstation was crowded with a stand-alone DVD writer, a digital scanner and stacks of CDs and DVDs. A neatly-lettered nameplate on his desk displayed his authority over the place.

Bansi was dressed in his patchy jeans and worn-out sky-blue T-shirt – his *uniform* of many years. He had no sense of style, and his choice of clothes made him appear more or less the same every day.

After dropping out of a computer programming course – which he had joined after dropping out of college – his life revolved around managing the cyber café and writing college project reports. Over time, he had mastered the art of writing assignments for students. Typically, each would make him a profit of more than five hundred rupees. By contrast, he earned only fifteen rupees per hour per cabin.

Bansi was buried behind his PC when Rahul interrupted. 'Bansi, you know, today I reached level six. I put in all my efforts to reach Kamsa's palace,' he started, as he extended two ten-rupee bills.

Bansi did not say anything. He picked up the logbook from his desk and ticked off Rahul's name against Cabin 18. The logbook had the visitor's name, ID, time of entry and every other detail mandated by the Secunderabad police sub-division.

'Cabin 18, that's two hours. Thirty rupees,' said Bansi in a clear voice.

'An hour and half only, please,' begged Rahul.

'You came at 9.00. Now it's 11.05. Two hours!'

Rahul looked around, as if searching for someone. 'Kanu would have taken only twenty. Where is Kanu? I saw him coming to the café.'

'Kanu didn't come. We are not here for charity!'

Not finding any relief, Rahul shouted, 'Kanu, Kanu!' The place fell silent. He called out again, as if to embarrass Bansi.

Bansi tried to take control of the situation, gesturing at Rahul to calm down. But before any words could be exchanged, Kanu emerged, seemingly from nowhere.

Kanu Vasukumar was a part owner of the café. Kids loved him because he allowed them extra gaming hours every time they visited the shop. He wore his button-down shirt with small front pockets – four buttons undone, revealing his plain, white cotton T-shirt. Otherwise, he too looked his usual, sporting a three-day stubble, spiked hair with a windswept look, headphone cables coiled around his neck, and an enormous wristwatch with multi-coloured beads that was on display as he held his flip-phone close to his ear.

'Okay, listen, I'll call you back. This work can wait,' Kanu spoke into his handset before sliding the phone into his sagging jeans pocket.

'You lost again, Rahul?' Kanu asked.

'Know what? I was misled by a strange-looking demon. There was this giant ape. I followed it and found Kamsa. But I had lost all my powers by then!' explained Rahul.

'But you *lost*, right?'

'I can try again tomorrow –'

'I'll do you a favour. I'll give you a cheat-sheet when you come back tomorrow.'

'Cheat-sheet? What's a cheat-sheet?'

'Normally, when you log into a game, the game communicates its rules to you. With the cheat-sheet, you can take control over the rules. You can override some of the original programming.'

'Wow!'

'Believe me, you'll be *the God*!'

'I can kill Kamsa?'

'Sure, you can! Okay, give me this.' Kanu collected the money that Rahul was holding. 'Next time when you come, don't forget to ask for the cheat-sheet!'

Rahul smiled. He was excited about his next chance to fight his enemy. Though he had lost the game, he was going home a winner.

Bansi, who was buried again in his project, did not make any effort to listen to Kanu's typical style of persuasion.

'Keep this,' said Kanu, handing over the money to Bansi.

'But its only twenty,' said Bansi.

'He is just a kid. You are a gamer too. You know how time flies.'

The girl sitting in Cabin 14 keenly following the conversation felt like supporting Kanu but was hesitant to strike up a conversation.

Bansi was not impressed.

'Okay, I'll deduct it from your account,' Bansi said.

Kanu smiled. 'Listen, I am busy coding. Can you order some food? From Marwaris. Maybe half an hour from now? I ask you now because I know I'll forget!' Kanu did not wait for Bansi to respond. He went straight to his special cabin where he would spend the afternoon with his computer.

The girl in Cabin 14 sighed as she watched Kanu go.

Kanu was a programmer and a self-styled hacker. Writing code and breaking into other computers was his life. Right from childhood, his computer gave him an opportunity to be himself. He connected with the world outside more easily through computer games and online chat rooms.

He was interested in making money as well.

Since his schooldays, Kanu had known how to exploit the booming pirate software market in Hyderabad. He replicated software available in the market, worth thousands of rupees, at a fraction of the original cost. He had the ability to modify internal registry files by writing specific keys or codes against what came bundled with the original software. His pirated computer software had a different set of markets.

Money started trickling in. He saved a portion of it to start his cyber café in partnership with his friend, Bansi. They named their start-up *MNR*, *Money-Not-Required*. Now, in its fourth year, MNR was all about generating money.

Back in his personal cabin, Kanu grabbed the mouse to open up a new window. His current assignment was to tweak existing code and customize a programme interface for a client. Tinkering with existing programming and reverse engineering in general was his strength.

He would start by understanding the target server that hosted the programme. He relied on his knowledge and tools to gain access to the target server by taking advantage of one of the built-in operating system flaws. Then he would keep a look out for the intended target server to analyse for vulnerabilities that could be further exploited. Choosing and configuring an exploit to take advantage of the remote server was always easy. The tricky part was to find ways to get the exploit executed inside the target computer that hosted the server, move files, secure data and clean up all traces so that the intrusion data wasn't detected.

Kanu was quick on his fingers. Text flew across his computer screen as if heavenly magic made instantaneous changes on it. For now, Kanu was in total control of his target system. He opened up another window, a hacked FTP server, and moved files from his current exploit. The computer displayed a message that read: Two hours remaining. *Job well done*, *time for lunch!*

Later that day, as Kanu and Bansi were finishing their lunch, Kanu saw an orange-haired man walk into the café. A girl in skin-tight jeans and a tank top hung on his arm. She looked simple but beautiful, without any makeup.

Is that Pankaj? Kanu thought as he tried to recollect his last encounter with him.

Pankaj Kumar was an old batchmate from the computer class of 1998. From early on, Pankaj was a key member of a team that was engaged in developing code for an offshore project headed by their guide Sachin Kelkar. Kelkar was a great coach and an industry veteran who coordinated several projects on behalf of the institute. He had complete knowledge of computer programming, but lacked the nuance required to break into others' computers. As a coach, he never approved of the use of tools such as port scanners, rootkits, log file cleanup, sniffers and a variety of other programmes that his students regularly used.

Kanu, on the other hand, was inquisitive. He was fearless when experimenting with a problem and redefining the source code. As a team, both Pankaj and Kanu allowed their guide Kelkar to undertake and execute any ambitious project.

But Pankaj was not a team player. He preferred working independently instead of collaborating with his peers. Often Pankaj would pass off others' projects as his own, including those of Kanu's, without acknowledging their efforts.

Kanu tried to walk over to the other side of the shop, eager to make his escape. *Orange hair! Orange, of all colours!*

But Pankaj spied him first. 'I want a cabin,' he demanded. 'How much do you charge? Looks like, you collect fifteen rupees.' Pankaj glanced at the pricing board. With a sly smile he said, 'I'll give you thirty!'

'You will have no cabin, even if you pay a hundred,' Bansi said angrily.

Realizing a showdown between them was certain, Kanu intervened. 'Pankaj, haven't I told you many times I am not giving away the code? If you are here to steal it from my system, you are wasting your time. What you want is *not* on any of the connected systems here.'

Pankaj did not respond. He looked at his girl as if she had dragged him into this game.

'Kanu, meet Rita,' he said. 'Rita, Kanu, my batchmate from old times!'

Kanu nodded as if to say 'Hi'. She gave him a friendly smile in return, completely clueless to what was transpiring between the men around her.

Pankaj and Kanu were both members of an underground elite hacking community called ICR PROXY. Pankaj went by the name of PuNk@1 in the underground circuit. Kanu was @DigitalGod. Through online threads, Pankaj had learnt that Kanu was writing a scanning tool that would enable its user to penetrate any system disguised as a genuine update of the native antivirus programme.

Kanu's multi-platform antivirus Remote Administration Tools (or RAT) allowed users backdoor access into a victim's computer without their knowledge or consent. The installation did not disturb the original programming architecture. In fact, the native antivirus programme considered it as part of its own function.

'Yes, I'm here for the remote tool. Think before you refuse,' warned Pankaj, 'you may regret it. I'll have it from my other sources eventually. You don't want that, do you?'

'What will you use it for? To spy on some innocent girl?' Kanu eyed the girl on Pankaj's arm.

'That's none of your concern. Look, I'll give you 20k. I have a customer who is offering around 40k. Fifty-fifty.'

'Is this for a pharma company you are working for?'

'That's none of your concern. It's not as if I can't crack the code. I just don't have time right now. Let's call it sixty-forty. Twenty-five yours, fifteen mine.'

'Eighty grand,' Kanu said, glancing at Bansi.

'Bullshit, no one will give you that kind of money!'

'80k. Final.'

Pankaj looked him in the eye. 'That's impossible. I'm leaving. But I'll get you for this.'

Kanu smiled. 'No hard feelings,' he said as the couple left silently.

That evening, Pankaj was busy figuring out other ways of acquiring the code. He was sipping tea at Masi's. Tucked away in a remote corner of the Osmania University campus, Masi's served the best Irani tea.

Rita stood by his side impatiently. 'Are we going for a movie or not?' she asked.

Pankaj did not respond and continued sipping from his cup. He looked at the kid serving tea. 'Another one for me.'

Rita sighed. 'Last week, you said we could go today. Now it's six already. Are we going?'

'I'm thinking.'

'You keep thinking. I'm going.'

'Okay, go.' Pankaj smirked.

'You are such an asshole. Before I go, I'll file a police complaint against you for hacking my e-mail account and blackmailing me into being with you.'

'What?'

'You hacked into my account. That's a crime.'

Pankaj set down his tea. *That's it! Kanu is into hacking. In fact, he often brags about his exploits. I've finally got him.* He turned to Rita and smiled. 'Listen, I'm coming with you. But you'll have to do me a favour.'

'What favour?'

'I know this policeman who registers complaints. And you have a complaint to file.'

Rita looked at him, unsure. But she did not focus on his words for too long. It was time for a movie!

TWO

5 December 2006

Kanu sped his two-stroke Yamaha RTZ 135cc to reach the CTC Complex. The bike was a rare find when he first purchased it, a second-hand marvel of the time. Now the lens cover on the turn signal was broken and the side of the tank had messages inspired by *Ninja Assassins* and *Cuban Revolution* to hide dents and other marks.

He parked his bike inside the CTC Complex compound area and went straight in to meet his business associate, Mukesh Aggarwal.

Mukesh was a middle-aged, computer-illiterate businessman who dealt in computer peripherals. Piles of computer hardware boxes, as well as computer peripherals, crammed the tiny space of his shop. He sat on one side of the room, wearing a semi-transparent, white designer shirt.

'Over there, at that counter,' Mukesh directed a customer, who barely managed to squeeze through the space between the mountains of boxes and Kanu.

Kanu took his time settling into the chair on the other side of the overstuffed desk. He waited before speaking to make sure that Mukesh was looking at him.

'Did the software I delivered last time have any problems?' Kanu asked.

Mukesh looked at him with a gentle smile. 'No problem at all. Sometimes I feel that if there were codes in our window shutters, you could break them open too! Kanu, you are bang on when it comes to computer cracks.'

'Thanks, Mukesh. You can rely on me.'

'*Ahh* ... I have one more job for you.' Mukesh pulled out a copy of a CD-ROM and placed it on the desk. 'If you can help me crack the code for this software – it's being sold in the market for 20,000 – I'll earn nothing less than 5,000 per copy. Don't worry, you will get a good share from it as well.'

'Consider it done.' Kanu nodded, not wanting to waste more time negotiating the deal. Mukesh leaned back in his chair, looking at the package on his desk.

'How many days will it take?'

'Five to six days, max.'

'Great.'

'Is there anything else –'

'For now, this is what I need. Here's the CD.' Mukesh slid the CD-ROM towards Kanu. 'Hold on,' he said, rummaging through his cabinet, 'I need to pay you for your last assignment. How much?'

'Your call.'

'Here, this is 10,000. Count it.'

'We are not in the counting business, Mukesh,' replied Kanu as he pocketed the money.

Kanu's phone rang as he climbed on his bike. It was Bansi.

'The police have raided our shop,' his friend's stricken voice came from the other side.

'Bansi? Raid? What kind of …' Kanu stopped mid-sentence. 'Hello?'

'They're taking our CPUs and hard discs. Come quick,' Bansi said.

'How did they find us?' His words came out harsh and urgent. He realized what he had said would upset Bansi further. 'I mean, what did we do wrong?' he added.

'I don't know. It doesn't make sense. Hurry.'

The line went dead.

Kanu kick-started his Yamaha and drove out of the compound in a fury.

As Kanu approached the café, he saw a police van and white motorbikes parked outside. Bloody hell! He studied the numbers on each license plate as he climbed off his bike.

When Kanu stepped inside, he saw a couple of uniformed policemen heading into the dimly-lit passage of the cyber café. They were quickly stacking computer CPUs and other equipment.

Kanu approached a policeman standing near the counter. 'What did we do?' he asked. 'Why are you taking away all this?'

The badge pinned on the uniform of the policeman read, Parthik Patel. Parthik was a young man in his mid-twenties who seemed anxious to finish his work and return to his place of comfort.

'You're Kanu? The owner of this cyber café?' Parthik asked.

'Yes.'

'We've come to pick you up. There is a complaint against you. We are taking your computers to scan through your documents. If you cooperate, we will let you go. We are not arresting you yet. You understand? Without evidence, we cannot arrest you. That depends on what we find.'

Kanu was steady, but his mind raced. *What files did I leave on my computer? What do these cops know?*

Bansi stood quietly behind Kanu, still unsure of the motive behind the raid. 'What's the charge?'

'Blackmailing a girl and hacking her e-mail account.'

'What?' Kanu sputtered. 'No! We would never do such a thing.'

Bansi intervened. 'Listen, we are not into hacking. We make college projects. That's all there is to it. There must be some mistake –'

'There is a written complaint against you, Kanu,' the policeman interrupted. 'Consider this as an investigation. If you follow us, we'll let you go. Do you understand?'

Kanu had no answer. He had often cracked open e-mails and gained unauthorized access, but the charge of blackmailing was wrong. He had never in his life blackmailed anyone. But he decided to remain silent.

The combing operation continued while Kanu was led into the waiting van.

At 2.20 p.m., the police van pulled up in front of the Gopalapuram police station in Secunderabad. It had a huge campus, spilling across the road to include a traffic control station on the other side.

Darshu Soni stood in front of the station, her phone tucked between her ear and shoulder. She had a notebook in one hand and a pen in the other. She seemed to be staring ahead at the police vehicles, as if studying the number plates. 'Okay, listen, there is an interesting development here. I think they have picked up a guy with loads of computers. Looks like an interesting story. Keep an anchor space for my report.' She signed off.

Darshu stood out among the crowd of tired-looking policemen. Her dark hair, pale skin and innocent good looks were a world away from the place she frequented to cover stories for her publication, the *Deccan Courier.*

Kanu stepped out of the van and trudged towards the police station, a few metres away from where Darshu stood.

A policeman escorted him. 'Behave properly. Agree to whatever Bada Babu says,' he muttered as he guided Kanu down the corridor to Bada Babu's office.

While walking through the passage, Kanu paused near a large, open room and listened carefully. He thought he recognized the voice inside. *Is that Pankaj?*

For sure, Pankaj was having a conversation with someone in the room.

Kanu stared in anger. *Did Pankaj plan this raid to get access to my computer? Bastard, he was offering me twenty grand. With ten grand, the best policeman can be bought.*

The constable shoved Kanu from behind. 'Keep moving!' he said.

The station office was nothing more than an old wooden table, a couple of chairs and few folders stacked in a metal rack. Inside Bada Babu's room, two men stood waiting. Kanu stood with them in silence.

'You run the computer shop on Rezimental Street?' Bada Babu asked.

'Yes,' said Kanu.

'Look, we don't have time for petty things like computer games, e-mail and all. There is a complaint against you in the Kachiguda station. Some girl says you've hacked her e-mail and blackmailed her.'

'Girl? What girl? That's not true.'

Bada Babu held out a copy of written complaint for Kanu to read. 'Here, this complaint is filed by Rita. Do you know her?'

'No, I don't know anyone named Rita. This is a set-up. I am being framed!'

'You can discuss that with the police sub-inspector in Kachiguda.'

'But I'm innocent!'

'Go to Kachiguda. They will tell you what to do.'

Outside the traffic control station, next to the Golden Jubilee tea joint, Darshu was talking to an old acquaintance, Parthik.

Parthik had been one of her most reliable sources. He filtered out unnecessary news, providing only information that made for a good story. He made his living around the edges by taking favours, mostly in cash. But for Darshu he was readily available at any time of the day.

'We conducted the raid at the MNR Cyber Café to nab this guy, Kanu Vasukumar. He is a well-known hacker. We have called him for questioning based on the complaint filed by a girl called Rita. She reported that her e-mail account was hacked,' Parthik informed.

'You mean to say, this guy hacks into computers and steals their data and e-mail IDs?' Darshu asked, furiously taking notes. 'How many computers have you seized?'

'Fifteen. He's *selling* this information to someone, I am sure.' Parthik watched the gorgeous scribbling on her pad with obvious interest.

Just then, they heard the ignition of a vehicle and the roar of an outdated van. A tall man and a uniformed constable were getting inside.

Shit! Are they leaving? She pulled out a digital camera from her handbag and pointed towards the oncoming vehicle, clicking till it was gone.

'I don't think your camera got a shot of him,' Parthik said.

'Don't worry, I'll be investigating it further.'

'Why don't you ask that man standing there? He knows more about computer crimes. The department hired him to look into what that other guy had.'

'That man in blue T-shirt, orange hair?' Darshu looked at the weird-looking guy.

'Yes, the guy with orange hair. His name is Pankaj. He is helping us trace the stolen data,' replied Parthik.

Darshu was halfway inside the station when she overheard the conversation between two middle-aged constables.

'Our newly recruited lad is a good friend of this lovely reporter,' said the first constable.

'In our day there were not many lady reporters. Or I would have married a reporter too!' replied the second with a big smile on his face.

The police station had never been the easiest place for a female journalist. Darshu ignored them and walked up to the man in the blue T-shirt.

'Your name is Pankaj, right?'

'Yeah,' replied Pankaj.

'I'm Darshu Soni from the *Deccan Courier.*'

'We tried to contact the girl who lodged the complaint against you. What's her name? Rita, I think,' said the sub-inspector in charge of the Kachiguda police station. 'Seems she's not available on her cell. You can write a declaration stating that the charges against you are false and we will let you go.'

'What exactly should I write?' asked Kanu.

'That you are not involved in computer theft. That you don't indulge in hacking and e-mail stealing.'

'To whom do I address the letter?'

'DSP–Kachiguda,' the policeman informed him. 'Listen, I spoke to Bada Babu. You will receive your computer, hard disc and your other stuff from Gopalapuram station after they have verified you're clean.'

'There is nothing in our computers, believe me.'

'I agree. Our team will search your computer files, but we still have to check. You understand?' said the policeman.

By this time, Bansi was also in the Kachiguda station, along with a bunch of his friends. The police personnel in general openly exploited such situations to extract money from innocent victims. Two thousand rupees quickly changed hands and the case was settled.

That evening Darshu sat in front of her monochrome monitor, feeling swamped by the written notes collected from different sources. Instead of writing, she decided to browse the wire. Her story was unlikely to be followed by the newswire, but she wanted to read other stories for inspiration.

After a while, she logged back in, uncertain how to begin. She looked around. There were two other reporters in the editorial department, busy with their work. Otherwise, the room was empty.

Just then, a middle-aged man dressed in a dark suit, bristling with quiet authority, entered the room. Gaurav Rathod was *the* celebrity journalist and editor-in-chief of the newspaper. He was famous for his newsgathering and editorial gigs. The blurb at the bottom of his column never failed to remind readers that he was an *award-winning journalist*. 'Ayesha told me that you are doing the anchor story?'

'Evening, sir!' Darshu turned to greet him. 'An Internet café owner, a young guy, apparently turned rogue, driven by profit. He hacks into other people's computers. The police rounded him up this afternoon.'

'Great! Do you have any photos to go along with the copy?'

'I clicked one. Doesn't look very sharp.' She extended her camera.

'This should be okay,' he said, squinting. 'About 400 words.'

'When do you want it?'

'Whenever you are ready with it.'

'I just came in to –'

'Take your time! I'll be here till 9.30.' The editor walked into his glass cabin in one corner of the office.

At 9.00 p.m., Bansi and Kanu were at the Gopalapuram station to collect the CPUs and hard discs seized by the police. There were five CPUs stacked in one corner, while the rest of them were inside the room.

'Should we call a taxi?' asked Bansi.

'How much did you pay the ... *policemen*?'

'Two thousand!' Bansi paused a moment before adding, 'I know who did this.'

'Yeah, me too.'

'Why would Pankaj keep playing such cheap tricks?'

'We'll discuss this later. We have to haul all of this back to the café.' Kanu zoomed away on his Yamaha and in no time came back with an auto rickshaw. They stuffed their wares inside and were gone.

THREE

6 December 2006

Pranjal Hazarika pushed opened the partially frosted glass door and stepped inside the sprawling office of Sathyamev Computer Services. He arrived early, as usual, to get a head start on the day. The one thing that he dreaded most of all was getting into an elevator with his boss.

The front office was deserted, except for two security guards, who doubled as the reception. As soon as Pranjal approached the newspaper stand, not far from the reception desk, both guards stood to attention to greet him.

Pranjal smiled and nodded. He was tall and lean, and wore formal trousers along with a full-sleeve shirt.

'Is there a letter for me?' he asked the security guards as he moved closer to the newspaper stand to pick up a copy of the *Deccan Courier.*

'Yes, sir. It's been delivered to your mail box,' said the older guard.

Pranjal nodded and walked towards the waiting elevator.

The corporate headquarters of Sathyamev Computer Services in Madhapur had been a hallmark of the city's emerging status as an information technology hub ever since the idea of Cyberabad Technopolis started taking shape in the early '90s. Its glistening, twenty-storey building towered over all other constructions in the vicinity. The penthouse had a window with a 360-degree view of the lush, green twenty-acre campus. A rock garden, equipped with an amphitheatre, adorned the landscape in front of the building. Across the garden, a dome-shaped state-of-the-art Sathyamev Learning Centre added to the beauty. Large and small Sathyamev offices were scattered across Hyderabad and Secunderabad, but the HQ was the only one that housed the company's famous penthouse office.

On reaching the eighteenth floor, Pranjal collected the newsletters and went straight to his cabin. As the chief information officer of Sathyamev, his routine included browsing through the closure reports and responding to the system-critical mail.

Pranjal studied the city supplement of the newspaper as he powered on his personal computer. An article on the front page caught his attention: *Hackers on the prowl in Hyderabad*. According to the article, a cyber café owner had compromised data of several top-notch companies ... including Sathyamev. *How could that be? Sathyamev files are with a hacker?* Pranjal thought. *This is a disaster.*

He read the article again:

HACKERS ON THE PROWL IN HYDERABAD
Darshu.Soni@DC.in.com

Hyderabad: He lurks within the undefined boundaries of the Internet, exploiting the vulnerabilities of a connected world most of us could never understand or learn. Some call him a hacker; others call him a cracker or a punk. Whatever you call him, he's the kind of person who revels in the glory of compromising computer data simply to prove a point or to get rich quick.

Meet twenty-two-year-old Kanu Vasukumar, who was called in for questioning at the Gopalapuram police station in Secunderabad. His crime: violation of cyber laws. Police files revealed he broke into a girl's personal e-mail ID and allegedly blackmailed her into submission. According to a police source, following the raid they conducted at his MNR Cyber Café, located on Rezimental Street, incriminating data was recovered from his seized computer hard drive. This included vital customer data of companies such as Sunrise Pharma, Sathyamev Computers, and Tajraj Hotels.

With secrecy a vital part of his work, the hacker – who goes by the handle @DigitalGod – has also collated a huge database of pirated software. It is believed that he sells this software to various vendors across the city.

'People living in an online world often lead a double life,' said Pankaj Kumar, an expert on online security. 'They may look normal, but these kinds of people just like to set fire to establishments and watch them burn. That's why they keep data of big companies. The idea is to humiliate them.'

With the rise in cyber attacks in the form of malware, Trojans and viruses, this incident has called into question the safety of our own online identities. 'Most professional and high-level hacks are never detected,' added Pankaj. 'We have to build additional capabilities by installing antivirus programmes in our systems, re-encoding passwords every month and storing important files in backup drives.'

Pranjal stood up and paced the room. Despite the air conditioning, his forehead was beaded with sweat, and his hands perspired as he grabbed the receiver to call his assistant.

'Did you see the paper?' Pranjal paused to listen. 'Okay, now tell me how far away is this Rezimental Street area from our office?'

Pranjal was beginning to recover from the initial shock of the article. 'Get me the details of MNR Cyber Café at once. Clear up the server room and start securing backup files. Someone must have stolen our backup files.' There was a moment of silence. 'You don't understand! *We are in big trouble*. Secure all your files. Report to me immediately. I will have to call HR and explain everything.'

Kanu was asleep when his cell phone buzzed. He answered it without even looking at the name displayed.

'What is it?' he mumbled.

'Your name has appeared in the *Deccan Courier*,' said the voice on the other end of the line.

'*Deccan Courier*? Okay, I'll check.' He yawned, rolled over, and went back to sleep.

Darshu got up early. Over a cup of coffee, she opened the paper and scanned through the *Deccan Courier* supplement *Hyderabad Courier,* which carried her story. She read the byline – Darshu Soni. For some reason, bylines always made her feel happy about being in print journalism.

She had landed in Hyderabad through sheer luck. In 2000, with the qualifying credentials of a higher secondary degree, she had applied for a scholarship at Loyola College of Journalism and was selected on the basis of a blog that she maintained. Soon, she began her college education, focusing more on freelance assignments than attending classes. As it turned out, she was more of a student-writer-at-work than a traditional student attending college. She spent most of her time writing features, corporate blogs and other such assignments.

In 2004, after having completed her undergraduate studies, she applied for a position at the *Deccan Courier*. She was again selected and recruited as a reporter. Tasks assigned to her ranged from writing for the gourmet section to attending press conferences.

But crime stories captivated her interest. The crime beat was both challenging and rewarding. She developed a devoted network of close friends who helped her get scoops on breaking stories. Her sources became her strength. In addition to this, reporting crime stories also meant flexible work hours. Her work schedule was now reduced to three to four hours a day, allowing her to focus on hobbies like learning Germanic languages.

Along with her roommate Ritika, Darshu had short-leased an apartment in Marredpally for three months, but they had stayed on for more than eight months. For two single women living independently in a city, this was not only the safest but also the most carefree apartment available.

'They ran my story without even editing it!' Darshu shouted. 'Ritika, where are you? What are you doing inside? Your coffee is getting cold!'

Ritika Patel was Darshu's college friend and roommate. Unlike her friend, Ritika was a self-proclaimed 'party animal'. After graduating with Darshu, she had worked as a management trainee in the corporate communication division of an MNC and was soon offered a job. She enjoyed her work as well as her salary, which more than covered her exuberant nightlife.

Ritika came out with a cup of coffee in one hand and a sandwich in the other. She frowned at Darshu's grip on the newspaper and found her roommate staring intently at the words.

'What's wrong with you?'

Darshu looked up. 'Did you see this?'

'No.' Ritika shook her head, laughing. 'It's not office hours yet.'

Darshu growled in frustration. 'What office hours? Reading can't be part of office hours. Look, our editor did not edit the copy!' She shook the newspaper for emphasis.

'Good for you! Must've been perfect, as usual.' Ritika lifted her brows as she sipped her coffee. Her roommate's perfectionism was as amusing as always.

Darshu ducked her head, dark hair concealing her features. 'I could have written it in a different way ...'

'Yes, Darshu. That's very good to know. Now, on to more important things.' She glanced at her. 'Did you get New Year's party passes for the Taj?'

'No.'

'No? I've been asking you to do it almost every day! There's hardly any time left! What am I supposed to do?'

'I can't really help, Ritika. You need four passes. Where will I get so many?'

'Okay, if not Taj, how about Baseraa?' Ritika hated settling for a smaller venue, but it would have to do.

'I'll try ...' Darshu said in a soft voice.

'Do you want me to talk to your boss? I'm good at that.' Ritika winked.

Darshu did not respond. Instead, she walked into the passageway that connected the balcony to the living room. She side-stepped around the coffee table and the sofa to reach for a wooden stool stored underneath the computer table. Then she powered on the CPU as she pulled out the stool.

'I said I'd try, and I will. Okay?' she called. 'Now, if you get ready, we can go early today.'

Ritika did not let her finish. 'Hmm, go early? Some important meeting with the cute new marketing manager, huh?'

'Shut up!'

Kanu stopped near a public telephone booth where newspapers were neatly laid out on a wooden cot. He parked his bike and pulled out a copy of the *Deccan Courier*. He could not locate the news in the daily or its city supplement. He reached for his mobile.

'Bansi, there is no news, *ra*!'

'It's on the front page, *ra*.'

'Front page! I thought some chindi news might have come ... Wow! Look at this!' Kanu exclaimed as he read his name and other details in the newspaper.

'First time in the newspaper, *ra*!' exclaimed Kanu. 'Our guru used to say: *Kam karneka aise ke paper mein photo aneko hona!*'

'The photo is of a van. Not you!'

'I am in the van, *ra*!'

It was business as usual for most Sathyamev Computer Services employees, but Pranjal sat inside the nineteenth floor conference room, sweaty and nervous. Samba Rajput, Sathyamev's chief operating officer, had summoned him for an urgent meeting about the newspaper report on the data breach.

Pranjal sat with Venkatesh Hari, his counterpart from the human resources department, who, in contrast to Pranjal, looked calm and relaxed. Venkatesh was an old-timer at Sathyamev and was the official spokesperson for the company. He was dressed in a well-tailored suit and looked youthful with cropped hair, chiseled features, and a body that spoke of regular trips to the gym.

Exactly at 11.00 a.m., Samba Rajput walked in with a glamorous female assistant in tow. Samba had thick, long hair and gray eyes. His dark leisure suit, white starched shirt and gray tie made him look quite distinguished.

Samba took a seat at the opposite end of the table, his face unresponsive and grave. After a few seconds, he shot a glance at his assistant.

'Sheena, can you set up the projector?' Samba looked hard at Pranjal and then at Venkatesh. 'This is not what we want to read about Sathyamev in the newspaper – this news report on the data breach. It's just not done. We have to get behind the story and find out the truth. But before we do that, our CEO would like to talk to you.'

Samba adjusted his chair closer to the table. 'Sheena, are we connected yet?'

At twenty-one, Sheena was eighteen years younger than her boss but was handy with all things technical. She did not reply or nod. Instead, she punched codes into a handheld device and spoke into the microphone on the conference table.

'Hi, this is Sheena from HQ. Am I audible?' she said. 'I have entered the codes.'

As the screen flickered, the shaky image of a frail-looking man wearing a pin-striped shirt, sitting on a lounge chair in a distant poolside luxury hotel, appeared.

The image stabilized and the slim figure converged into the renowned face they had known for many years: Rana Rajput. The image was not just a projection of a man sitting far away – to his men, Rana mirrored the image of an enlightened man.

Rana loved to give the impression of being able to transcend physical distances; he wanted to be seen as a man who could do anything. He was sitting outside a luxury hotel in some foreign country and also inside a conference room in Sathyamev's headquarters at the same time.

Rana had been a father figure to the entire information technology industry that had mushroomed in and around Cyberabad. 'As a captain of the outsourcing industry,' the chief minister of Andhra Pradesh once gloated in his IT Conclave inaugural address, 'Rana Rajput is no less than a *legend*.'

Rana put on his spectacles and looked down at his men, searing contempt visible in his eyes. 'Gentlemen, give me updates. Only bullet points!'

Terrified, Pranjal began mumbling. 'Sir, we have started ... have got to ... come to know ... why ... it happened. How it happened ...'

Venkatesh took over. Leaning towards the microphone, he outlined the work in progress. 'We have pieced together information about the data breach. The person in question is a small-timer from Rezimental Street. Our sources in the police department have confirmed that they found a few files on Sathyamev.'

'What files?' the voice from the speaker asked.

'It's a log – customers log and three years' worth of declared financial statements. I've not seen it. But there could be more.'

'Pranjal, how did this breach happen?'

Venkatesh did not let Pranjal speak. 'Seems that an auditor's laptop must have gone out to be serviced to these guys. We are strict on RSA security installations. All our laptops are secured, but auditors do not comply with our standards. They have access to all our files, and someone must have left his laptop with these guys. Our investigation is ongoing. You will get a report by the evening.'

'Can you check what can be done to plug this auditor thing? Pranjal, let me know. Keep it in bullet points.'

'Yes sir,' agreed Pranjal. He looked relieved.

Samba glared at him, as if to say *thank you* and *leave the room*. He was utterly disappointed by the way his CIO had handled the crisis. Pranjal collected his papers and walked out quietly. As he was leaving, he overheard Venkatesh take up another topic.

'Sir, the discrepancy in recruitment figures – and there are thousands of *unknown* employees – is mainly due to a mismatch with campus placements. Even I don't know how these figures are tallied. There is something wrong with –'

Then the door closed behind him.

Darshu reached her office at 11.30 a.m. and was greeted by Ayesha Pathan, her supervisor. Ayesha occupied the seat allocated to Darshu and tapped away at the keyboard. Darshu rolled her eyes and put her hands on her hips, as if to scare away her boss from the seat.

'There is no security in this place. Anyone can access my computer!' Darshu said.

'I've told you many times it's all interconnected. And I like this keyboard!' Ayesha replied. 'By the way, your copy on the computer crime was good. You should dig deeper. Collect evidence on how these hacker groups leave no trails behind. It's kind of magical, isn't it?'

'I know!'

'I was discussing this with Gaurav. He said he received a call from our Delhi office, and he's going to call you about it.'

'Really? The Delhi office!'

'Yes.'

'Wow! I didn't think this was such a big story.'

That afternoon, Darshu began her investigation. She started with Google. *Computer + crime*. The results listed articles from Kevin Mitchnik's exploits to the involvement of Russian mafia in the identity theft business. Nothing terribly useful, but considering her lack of knowledge on the matter, it was informative. She continued her quest with *computer + hackers*, *computer + white crime*, *hacker + getting rich*, *hacking + Hyderabad*.

For about an hour, Darshu struggled to make sense of the articles. *This is no use,* she finally thought. *I can get better information from the place where it all started. MNR Internet Café + Secunderabad*. Google's reply: *Did you mean MNR Cyber Café?*

Hell, yes!

It took about fifteen minutes to reach Rezimental Street and locate MNR Cyber Café. She liked the uncluttered interior and the seating arrangements. The soothing background score made her feel at ease. The cubicles in the café were arranged in the centre, in a double H-shaped wooden framework. Cabins were located in the corners of the shop. They were fitted with sliding doors for privacy. Instructions on the cabins read: *Do Not Load Pornographic Sites. Please, We Are Hyderabadis!* A printed poster plastered nearby listed the charges.

She looked around, hoping to find someone. A girl, who seemed like a customer, was standing some feet away. 'There's no one at the reception desk?' Darshu asked her.

A voice from underneath the desk startled her.

'Right here, at your service,' shouted Kanu as he emerged with printer cables in one hand and cartridges in the other. 'Sorry about that. The printers are acting up. Happens all the time. Can you give me two more minutes?'

She knew right away the man with the cables and cartridges was her quarry. How could such an attractive young man be a major hacker? And a repair man for printers? Instinctively, she felt the need to twirl her hair, to touch it. She was surprised by the attraction she felt for this guy. *What is this? Criminals are not my type!*

Kanu opened the printer tray and arranged the papers in the proper order. In no time, the printer lit up and started churning out documents. The college girl looked excited. She began piecing papers together.

'That's not the correct order,' Kanu said, taking hold of the papers.

'Give me that,' the girl said teasingly. Clearly, Darshu wasn't the only one taken with his good looks. 'You take this.' She handed another set of papers to him as she crossed over to the printer, gently brushing her hands against his arm.

Kanu was flushed.

'Do you have time to talk?' Darshu asked.

'Yes, in ten minutes. Please have a seat,' he said, pointing to the visitors' chair.

Darshu felt like she was kept waiting much longer than ten minutes while Kanu continued arranging the girl's report. And the annexures. And the graphs. *How difficult could it be to put one report in order? I bet his smile makes this place veeeery popular among college girls. He's probably like a rockstar, always surrounded by cheering college girls, messy hair and all!*

Tired of watching the show, she pulled out her pad and started scribbling. '*Expected waiting period – 10 minutes,*' she noted. '*Nice Music. Tempting ambience.*' She looked around for details. A message that caught her attention read: *Be Cyber Smart.* The sign ended with a call to join *the good fight against cyber crime.* A website, e-mail address and telephone number were provided for further assistance. She noted the details in her pad. While she scribbled, she watched how the girl leaned over him. *As if it was difficult to face the monitor from any other direction.* She had her hand on his and was pointing the cursor to the screen.

'*Orange and purple walls?*' Darshu continued to write. '*Playful colours. I always wanted to have our apartment painted like this. Will it look nice in my room? No! The girl is looking more nervous now. God! Is she going to faint or what? What's wrong with her?*'

After twenty minutes, Darshu realized the girl had finished her work and was on the way out. *Finally.*

Darshu stared at Kanu for a moment, then stood up, notepad in her hand. 'You seem to have a lot of work to do,' she started. 'Could you spare some time for my report as well?'

'Yeah, that's our bread and butter. Something on a floppy drive or a disc?' he asked.

'Yes, actually, I am here to write a report. But I don't have a disc.'

'No problem – I can help you write it. Have you prepared anything for the project?'

'Project? No, I'm *not* here for a college project. I am Darshu Soni from the *Deccan Courier* and I have a few questions for you.'

Minutes later, Darshu stood outside the café, phone in hand. 'He kicked me out!' she exclaimed, her voice trembling. She took a deep breath, trying to calm herself, but when she spoke again, her voice still carried a tremor. 'What am I supposed to do now?'

She pressed her palm to her other ear. 'What? No. I was polite. He said that he is not *interested*. Yes, I requested. Listen, I am just down the street from MNR Cyber Café. Can you please come?' She twirled her hair and then pulled at it, frowning.

Pranjal sat staring at his *Action Taken Report*. Time was running out. The data breach incident was unexpected and by far exceeded his worst fears. He picked up the phone to call his assistant.

'What's the status?' He paused to listen. 'Good. Give me the updates as soon as the hard-disc is secured.'

He heaved a sigh of relief before calling Venkatesh. 'Hello, Venkatesh, this is Pranjal. I believe the Internet connection to the hacker's café has been disconnected. Their computers and hard discs will be wiped clean by the evening. SISI Security men have been tasked with this job. We'll get you the report as planned.'

'Did you speak to the editor of the newspaper?' Venkatesh asked.

'Am I supposed to talk to the editor *as well*?' The shrill tone of his voice belied his notion that he had everything under control.

'Don't bother. I'll do that,' Venkatesh said coldly.

'Okay ... are you sure?' Pranjal asked.

'Yes,' Venkatesh snapped and hung up.

Hovering outside the cyber café, Darshu realized that her curt approach might have been the reason for Kanu's instant rebuff. She was not prepared to tackle the situation. Usually people welcomed reporters who wanted to write profiles about them. *This guy looked so cool. What could have happened? Was it because his ISP got snapped and there was no Internet connection? But what have I got to do with the Internet?*

She walked towards Abdul Bakery across the road, which looked more like a small joint than a proper restaurant. She needed a cup of tea to settle her nerves. *It's not rejection for the sake of rejection,* she reminded herself.

A little later, Ritika emerged from an auto rickshaw. As she crossed the busy street, Darshu noticed for the first time that her friend was a stunner. Her hair, her shape, her face. *Stunner and my BFF! She is always there in the time of crisis.*

'What happened?' Ritika asked, pulling up a chair next to Darshu. She signalled to the man at the counter staring at her. 'One more coffee, please,' she smiled.

'Nothing. He's busy with college girls, and I'm left without work. Look, two more girls are walking in. They must be coming in for college reports.'

'Who is busy with girls? Darshu, what are you saying?'

'Remember the hacker story? That story I did about a hacker? Today's pullout? So I went inside for an interview –'

'– and there were girls?'

'Yeah, I wanted to know about his work. Looks like he does girls – I mean, college reports for girls.'

'So, what can I do? Why did you call me, Darshu?' asked Ritika.

'Do me a favour. Can you go in and get me some notes? Anything. Say you want to make a college report or something.'

'Okay ...'

'I blew my chance. My only hope is you! I don't know any other hackers for this story.'

'Tell me,' Ritika said, a smile forming on her lips. 'Are you are getting me the passes for Christmas and New Year?'

'Hell, yes. Now listen. If he does answer your questions, take at least one photo of him. That should do.'

Ritika sipped her coffee, carefully observing the shop. Suddenly, Kanu walked out towards his bike.

'Is that the one? The handsome guy starting up his bike?'

'Yes!'

'Damn! He looks yum!' Ritika said, staring curiously in the direction of the bike. 'Come, let's go.'

'Where?'

'You want your story or not? Look, he's gone. The line is clear.'

Ritika and Darshu walked towards the cyber café. As they entered, Bansi was talking to two girls. They were waiting for the Internet connection to start working on their projects.

Ritika did not wait for the girl to finish. 'Hi, I have to work on a report. You create college reports for student projects, right?'

Bansi was used to pushy customers. Besides, this girl was beautiful. 'What's the subject?' he asked.

'Water bodies. It's about agriculture and healthcare in rural Madhya Pradesh.'

'Let me check.' Bansi looked into his system. 'I have a complete dataset for, um, WHO, ITCC, Darpan, and the Government of India. You want more on this topic?'

'There's more?'

'Give me a minute.' Bansi paused for a few seconds before he punched a few key words – *Madhya Pradesh + reports* – into the search bar. A list of folders and documents came up. The result included studies from WHO, the state government, health foundations, ITCC and a few NGOs.

'Wow! This is great! Honestly, this is exactly what I have been searching for.'

'Please have a seat,' Bansi added, pushing a wooden stool towards her.

'Where do you get your information?'

'Government websites and corporate FTP. We hack into the systems. Did you see today's paper? Our café's name is mentioned.'

'Really?' Darshu's breath quickened.

'Information shouldn't be confidential in the first place. So we hack. We make it public. For free. These research projects are sponsored by the state, funded by public money. Yet they are hidden from most. Look here,' he said, pointing to a board. 'We provide information for free.'

'Do you have any information on community-level check dams and agro-forestry?' asked Ritika.

'How do you spell it?'

'What check dam? C-H-E-C-K-D-A-M.'

Bansi typed the text and hit *Enter*. The screen displayed five research papers and a few government reports on the subject.

'Wow! Can I get this information? How much do I have to pay?'

'Just the cost for printing. The information is free!'

'I can't tell you how lucky I feel. I've been searching for this information for years!' Ritika turned and looked at Darshu as if to say *thank you*.

Darshu interrupted the conversation. 'You hack into private computers and government databases? Isn't that illegal?'

'Yes. But information should be free. Did you know our government maintains many datasets? Why should these be hidden?'

'Really?'

'Yes. Hiding information is illegal. Carrying out research using public money and not making it public – that's illegal. Hacking and putting it out in the public domain – that's called *public service*!'

'Do you make money from it?'

'Know what? We don't profit a single rupee from it.'

'So you do this alone?' asked Darshu.

'No, I don't do any hacking. It's my business partner. His name is Kanu. You must come meet him someday. He must have gone to the NIIIT Institute. That's our place.'

'NIIIT – the computer coaching centre in CTC Complex?' Darshu asked.

'Bang on!'

Darshu was speechless. She'd had a fairly low opinion of hackers before, but the truth might be entirely different.

Just then two rugged, heavily-built, armed men walked in with SISI Security badges neatly stitched to their uniforms. One of the men was a tad taller, but both were big and packed with muscle.

They came straight to the counter. Without bothering to ask Bansi's name or introduce themselves, the hulk said, 'I want you to show me all the folders where the Sathyamev files are stored.'

Is this happening because of my report? Darshu wondered in panic. She grabbed Ritika's hand and held it tightly.

'Can you tell me who you are?' asked Bansi. He tried to stand up but they pushed him back into his seat. 'We have deleted all the files. There is no file on Sathyamev,' Bansi muttered.

'Either you show us where the file is stored –'

'Look, this is the hard disc where all files are stored. E Drive.' He pointed at the CPU. 'It's not in here.'

The taller man crouched to have a proper look at the screen. 'Okay, so this is your E Drive.' He pulled out a brick-sized magnetic tool and placed it on the table. 'This magnetic strip will wipe your data forever. Is there anything important you want to save from this computer? *Do it now.* I'll give you two minutes.'

Frightened, Darshu and Ritika crept out, as Bansi tried to salvage a few files to a floppy disc.

Outside, the girls hurried down Rezimental Street without speaking. They were afraid, and also feeling guilty for having done nothing to help Bansi.

'They bullied the poor guy into submission. Now I won't get those reports on community-level check dams!' lamented Ritika.

'You are always worried about yourself. Think of that guy!'

'Yeah, and it's all because of you.'

'I only did the reporting. Besides, how was I to know what kind of work they're into?'

'Say whatever you want to say in your defence. By now, they must have wiped out all the records on check dams and agro-forestry.'

They were near Darshu's office.

'Are you coming in or what?' asked Darshu.

'No, I'm going home,' Ritika said, her lips pressed together in anger. Then she turned and walked away, leaving Darshu alone in the night.

FOUR

7–20 December 2006

The next day, Darshu decided to visit the CTC Complex in Secunderabad that housed computer hardware shops, service centres, and training points, including the NIIIT Institute.

She walked all the way to the fifth floor only to find one weary guard sitting in an empty classroom. He had his feet up on the desk, but he quickly spun around to greet the visitor.

Darshu took her time to react, unsure if he was the right person to talk to on the specific subject.

'Isn't this the NIIIT office?' Darshu asked.

'No, this is our classroom. Our office is downstairs. First floor – B 42.'

'That's where Mr Kelkar sits, right?'

'That's right. Guru Kelkar sits in the first-floor office. But he must be busy now.'

'Okay, can you help me get some information ...?'

'Information? What information?'

'Do you know anything about Kanu, Pankaj, Bansi and the others?'

'Do I?' the guard smiled. 'They were from the first batch of NIIIT graduates.' The guard straightened up to offer her every little secret he had known about the millennium batch. 'Wait until you hear this!' he said.

At the NIIIT head office on the first floor, Kelkar sat facing a monitor. A large banner behind him, with a picture of graduating students throwing their caps in celebration, made him appear small. He was, in fact, a tall, middle-aged man wearing navy-blue trousers and a starched, white shirt.

Darshu introduced herself with her visiting card as she entered the office, then began explaining the purpose of her visit. But Kelkar looked uninterested.

'Can you give me five more minutes? I'll finish this and get back to you,' he said.

'Sure.'

Darshu looked around. The coffee mug on his table had NIIIT printed on it in neat letters. NIIIT was also inscribed at the bottom of the monitor. The same logo resurfaced on the newspaper stand, notice board, photo frames and certificates. *Yeah, NIIIT it is!*

After some time Kelkar was ready to talk. 'Tell me, Darshu, what brings you here?'

'I came here to know more about the NIIIT millennium batch. I met your students, Kanu and

Pankaj.' Darshu placed her notepad on the table and pulled out a pen as she continued with her questions. 'Based on the information I've gathered, it seems that your students specialize in hacking.' She paused to assess his reaction.

Kelkar was unmoved. 'Go on.'

'Is there any specific course on hacking? I mean, how and why do your students start hacking? Is there something that can stop them? You know, like a good job or something?'

By this time, she had lost Kelkar's attention again. He was focused on his computer. 'So what do you want from me, Darshu?'

Darshu realized she must have been too vague in her questions. She thought for a while. 'Okay, why do your students hack into others' computers? Does it not reflect badly on the institute and their teachers?'

Kelkar finally seemed ready to listen. 'When students come here, we don't know what kind of futures they have. Both Kanu and Pankaj were bright when they joined. They were creative. They had passion. Sometimes skilled people need their own space and work atmosphere to bring out the best in them. Corporates cannot provide them that. Does that answer your question?'

'Why become a hacker? I mean, by hacking into others' computers and stealing information or trading secret files, aren't they committing crimes?'

'It depends on how you look at it. All good programmers are hackers. Being a hacker is a virtue. They have this ability to reframe the basic premise of a programme and seek a different solution to the problem.' He stared at her pen and paper. 'Are you getting this?'

'Yes, please continue.'

'Kanu was my best student. Writing a compiler came easy to him. Not because I taught him, but because he found it interesting. But his programmes had no customers in the real, applied world.'

'And what is a compiler?'

'I'll give you an example. Kanu's work is mostly based on abstract subjects, such as writing programmes for unmanned aerial vehicles or drones. Have you heard about drones?'

'No.'

'Have you heard about autonomous cars or the hackathon to write tools for building applications that could run a self-driving car?'

'No.'

'My dear friend, you are very new to this field. You should have done a refresher's course to understand our subject.'

She tried to apologize. 'I am sorry, my knowledge of computer programming is rather limited ...'

'Not at all – very kind of you to have come here to find the answers. But let me conclude by saying that the satisfaction of working on any independent project is immense, far more than earning a good salary in a big firm.'

'Onc final question. I want to know about Pankaj. I am told he is into hacking to profit himself –'

'Pankaj has his own agenda. I do not approve of his style of working. But there's much more that he can do.'

The man's answers had only raised more questions. Darshu was ill-prepared to follow up. Prominent on her notepad were words such as 'Autonomous car?' and 'Drones?' *What has hacking to do with autonomous cars and drones?* She returned to her office more confused than ever.

After finishing a write-up based on a press conference, Darshu walked all the way home. She had never worked on such a complicated and tricky assignment before. She turned to Ritika for suggestions.

Ritika was dressed for the night in a black T-shirt and shorts. She had occupied the couch for the greater part of the day watching a TV show and was not over with it yet. Darshu put her bag on a chair and sat on the little space that was left on the sofa.

'I went to NIIIT today to meet Kelkar. I think I made a mistake reporting that hacker story. Perhaps the police took money from Pankaj to seize computers from MNR Cyber Café. Then he disappeared. The guard at NIIIT also told me as much.'

There was no response. Her friend was engrossed in the programme.

'Rits, are you even listening? My story on the cyber café and hacking has backfired!' Darshu stood up and turned off the TV.

'What? Backfired?' shouted Ritika.

'It seems I was reporting the wrong side of the story,' Darshu said, her voice laced with sadness. 'That café owner is not a bad guy.'

'Listen, I know about it as well. I went back there to get my data. He is really bright.'

'Who's bright?'

'Kanu. He seemed upset that the incident you reported was so, ah, incorrect. But, you know, I spoke to him politely. Made him realize you were only doing your work. I'll bet he was upset with those two guys. They wiped the hard disc totally clean. Luckily, they had a backup of all their data. He said he would help me.'

'What did you tell him about me?' she prodded her friend. *Why do I care so much?*

'Nothing much. That you felt sorry.'

'And what did he say?'

'He is cool. It's the government research work I'm more worried about. Let's see how it goes.' Ritika's face lit up as she explained her project.

Darshu took a deep breath. 'This is going to be a long and complicated story without any closure. You know corporate people like Sathyamev have such muscle power, they can make even the editor crawl on their knees.'

'Why? What happened?'

'Gaurav called. He said that we might have to issue a corrigendum to the story. It seems the reporting was incorrect.'

The following day, Darshu was already at her desk when the other reporters began to arrive. She was busy typing out a story when Ayesha came up to her. She had a note in her hand and didn't look very happy.

'Darshu, we'll have to run a corrigendum to the hacking news.'

'Yeah, Gaurav told me. I filed a note. You can check in my recent documents.'

'The police confirmed that the company's name was wrongly mentioned. Clearly, giving out the company's name was a bad idea. And your source is unreliable. We must be careful when reporting.'

'I understand. I should have cross-checked with the company before writing about it.'

Deep inside, Darshu felt a portion of the blame was also on the editors – two levels of them – since they allowed the copy to get published exactly the way she had written it. But she did not say anything.

Ayesha held a few papers in her hand. 'This release too must go. Can you send me all the content?'

Darshu nodded and started typing. After finishing her work, she considered calling Ritika. It was unlikely Ritika would be at the cyber café, yet she wished just that.

At 3.00 p.m., Darshu was near the cyber café, unsure of what she was planning to do. She stood there, staring at the door. She wanted to apologize for fiddling in the hacking story with her half-baked report. She felt a strong urge to right the wrong. And perhaps to see Kanu.

She was trying to sneak a peek through the glass door when she felt someone tapping her shoulder.

Kanu was dressed in his trademark buttoned-down shirt over a faded pair of jeans with white headphones coiled around his neck. Suddenly, she felt a paralysing fear at having to talk to him.

'Hi,' her voice trembled.

'Hi,' said Kanu. 'Are you looking for someone?'

'Yes,' she said, and then stopped.

'Anything new you want to write about today?'

She gathered her wits enough to say, 'No. I was searching for Ritika. Have you seen her?'

'Yeah, she came and left. Why? Didn't she tell you that?'

'Maybe she did.' Darshu fumbled to reach her phone, hidden somewhere in her bag. *Damn this mobile. Now where is it?* When she found it, she scanned her messages. *There it is: Ritika.*

He stood still, eyeing her patiently. 'If you are looking for an interview, or thinking of writing about underground networks of the hacking community, you will not get any information here. Is that clear?'

Darshu had the handset glued to her ear. 'Um, no.'

'What?'

'It's not connecting. The line –'

'Why don't you do some other stories? There, the pavement is a mcss in this city. Why don't you do a story on that?'

'I made a mistake in the way I reported that story. I did the wrong thing by not getting your side of the matter.' She looked helplessly apologetic as she said these words.

Kanu hesitated for a moment, then smiled. 'Don't bother. We are used to such criticism.'

Her mobile buzzed.

'Hi, Darshu. You called me? Hello? Are you there?' Ritika was on the line.

'I was looking for you at the café,' said Darshu.

'Are you still there? Wait, I'll join you.'

'Join me? Yes, please do.'

Kanu invited her inside the cyber café. The place was filled with college students moving in and out of the square open space near the counter. The cabins were filling in fast. Bansi, who was at the counter, gave the charge to Kanu and went back to work.

'I'm working on this project for your friend,' Kanu reminded his guest.

'On check dams?' she asked.

'Ah! You seem to know! There've been so many studies on community check dam work, but reporting is always a problem. I feel passionately for such causes, you see.'

'Yeah.'

'We dig out reports funded by governments or state-sponsored universities. And know what? We can easily break in and gain access to such papers. Others can't. For me, it's important that all information must be freely available to all people, not just the privileged and wealthy.'

'I agree.'

'Do you? Really?'

'I know you won't believe this, but I told the same thing to Ritika. About the information thing –'

Kanu shook his head. He was unwilling to accept her explanation. After a while, Darshu asked, 'Do you have a cabin I can use?'

'I don't think we have any free. Here, you can use my computer.' Kanu checked his register. 'I usually don't allow people to use it. But you can. It's the one to the left – at the extreme end.'

'Thank you!' Darshu smiled.

'You are a journalist, Darshu. Now, don't dig too deep into my files.'

He winked.

While working on his computer, she realized Kanu's defining quality was his openness. *Why else would he give his private computer to me? A reporter?* The desktop icons on his system – agriculture research database, university research database – indicated his interest in making information freely available to all. There were no hidden agendas.

It did not take long for Ritika to reach the cyber café. She headed straight to Kanu. She extended her hand but it was not a mere handshake. It lingered.

'Is Darshu here?' she asked.

'Yeah, she's in my cabin. At the extreme end,' Kanu said, pointing.

Ritika did not bother to move. Perhaps she didn't want to disturb Darshu. Perhaps she didn't want to go anywhere. She dialled Darshu's number.

'Yeah, I am in the café. Why don't you come out?'

'Give me a minute,' Darshu answered, 'I am checking my e-mail.' Her voice was audible to everyone.

When Darshu emerged, it appeared as if Ritika was using her charms to lure Kanu. He was laughing heartily with Ritika. Their body language seemed *borderline* inappropriate to Darshu.

'Are we done with the report?' she butted in.

'Yeah, we are getting the printout,' Ritika said.

'Oh, printouts.' Darshu was reminded of her first visit to the place.

'Who knows if someone walks in to wipe the hard disc clean,' said Ritika.

'*Again!*' added Kanu.

Darshu was least amused by their banter. 'I know I owe you an apology, Kanu. I will correct this someday.'

Later, Darshu and Ritika stood outside, discussing something that mattered to them both.

'What was that? You were flirting with him!' Darshu exclaimed.

'What's wrong with you, Darshu? He is such an eye-candy! And so cooperative.'

'You know, Ritika, this guy is someone very dark.'

'That's so rare,' Ritika laughed. 'Handsome and *dark*!'

Darshu was speechless for a while. 'I mean dark in the sense, D-A-R-K. Shady. I am telling Ritwik about this.'

'Go tell him. He is too busy with someone else.'

'Poor Ritwik. Such a jerk, actually both of you are! I never liked him in the first place. So are you dumping him?'

'Kanu said he will get a case study on agro-forestry!'

'I asked you something,' Darshu insisted. 'About Ritwik?'

'No, for God's sake, why would I dump Ritwik?'

'Then what was that *inside*?'

'I told you, he said he'll get a case study on agro-forestry tomorrow.'

'Yeah, he will do anything for you. I don't know how you do it. I need to learn a trick or two from you!'

At 10.00 p.m. that night, Darshu saw a used wireless CDMA phone on the sofa of their living room. She studied the device closely. *Where does Ritika get all these freebies? Garage sale?* She concluded Ritika must have borrowed it to make long-distance calls to her boyfriend. It was late in the night. She went to her room.

In the morning, Darshu woke up to the sound of chatter coming from the living room. Ritika and Kanu seemed to be connecting the wireless CDMA phone to their computer. *Is that an amplifier attached to the phone?* The ugly-looking electronic device had two wires connecting the phone and the computer.

'What's happening in here?' Darshu asked.

'We are getting Internet!' Ritika replied.

'You're still on Windows 98. That must be slow. I'll get you the best pirated Windows XP,' said Kanu.

'A pirated copy!' Ritika squealed. She lived for a rush.

'Remember, this is a 56k modem. It's running on WLL technology. Not many people know this device can double up as a router. Remember, this is Windows 98, so it can slow things down. But I am installing it anyway.' Kanu was busy setting up the device.

Darshu realized her presence was not required. Blushing, she went back to her room.

After establishing the connection, Kanu looked at Ritika and pointed to the monitor that was loading a webpage on the browser. Ritika reached for the mouse and smiled as she saw another page coming up on the screen.

'Wow! Thank you so much!' she said.

'Any time! Got to go,' he said.

'I think you should meet Darshu before leaving.' Ritika shouted at the top of her voice, 'Darshu, the Internet is working! Kanu wants to say bye to you.'

'Okay, bye!' Darshu shouted back.

Kanu smiled and was gone.

Ritika closed the door and came back to check her computer. The web browser was slowly loading text and images when Darshu walked in.

'Aren't you guys going way too fast?' asked Darshu.

'Look, the Internet is working,' said Ritika.

'Why do you keep changing the subject?'

'Going fast? What do you mean by *fast*?'

'You invited him to our apartment.'

'How else do you think he could hook up our Internet connection?'

'Did you ask for it? Or is he giving it away just like that?'

'I paid 400. In the market, it's selling for just 100 bucks. "Monsoon Hungama Offer", remember? That guy is smart. He made a profit of 300 per cent on this sale. He said, use it as long as you want, then *throw* it away.'

'Yeah, I know it's illegal. And now he can easily hack into our computer and get our passwords!'

'Darshu, grow up!'

Darshu stared at the monitor, shocked. 'Did you see that? My files are already gone!'

'I put away all your files in the "Desktop Darshu" folder. Look, here!'

Darshu did not say anything.

The next day, instead of going to office, Darshu showed up at Kanu's cyber café first. She had her reason for the visit. Kanu was cleaning up the place when he saw Darshu walk in.

'You looking for Ritika again?' asked Kanu.

'No, I came to see you,' she replied.

'Me? No, I am not available.'

'Seriously, why did you leave an *illegal* WLL phone at our home? Are you trying to get your revenge or something?'

'Revenge? Hey, calm down.'

'I know how these phones are procured. You must have given wrong addresses, wrong telephone bills. They are all *illegal*.'

'Why do you consider everything *illegal*?'

'Because, it's illegal, that's why. Ritika said we could use the phone as long as we want, then throw it away. *Why throw it away?* She is very innocent. She does not know all her phone calls can be tracked.'

'You take white-collar crime way too seriously. Where do you get all this information from?'

'Does that matter?'

'Yes. Everyone around here has a WLL phone. The technology is simple. While others obtain them by producing fake electricity bills, we have them through our shop's address.'

'Do whatever you do. But please take away your illegal telephone.'

'Believe me, it's not illegal. It was lying around. That's why I gave it to her.' He shook his head in frustration.

At Sathyamev, Pranjal was busy collecting the printed pages of the *Action Taken Report*. The document contained a list of activities undertaken in the wake of the data breach reported in the *Deccan Courier*. When the report had been mailed to Samba Rajput, he was utterly disappointed with his team.

Many questions remain unanswered, he thundered at them. *How can we miss out naming the culprit? Did he store information only for fun or is this his usual business? What value does this information have in the outside world? Are there any customers for Sathyamev's data?*

The report was unacceptable.

Samba summoned Venkatesh to his office. 'Do you understand the importance of getting the correct news to our CEO? No, you don't. This report is useless.'

When Venkatesh read the report, he agreed with his boss. 'I will handle this issue myself,' he assured Samba. 'I thought Pranjal would have taken corrective actions.'

Samba nodded. 'Venkatesh, you have our SISI team at your disposal. Get our men to dig out every detail about this cyber café guy. But make sure to tell them to be subtle, you know, without fiddling or becoming too obvious.'

'Sure,' replied Venkatesh grimly.

Darshu left the *Deccan Courier* office at 6.30 that evening. She took the stairs down to the ground floor and spent the next five minutes walking along the footpath to reach St Mary's Church, close to the ITCC office. She was aware Ritika would have gone out with her office friends. Yet she dialled her number.

'I am outside your office, next to the exit gate of the church. Where are you?' Darshu asked.

'I am in Banjara. Something important?' Ritika replied.

'No, nothing. See you at home.'

'Enjoy *madi*!'

The ecstatic reply from the other end did not surprise her. It was Saturday evening after all. Darshu decided to go home and finish her blog.

Back in the apartment, she booted up her computer. The Internet dial-up icon was a new addition to the desktop shortcut menu. She double-clicked the icon. In no time, a new window popped open on the screen with the system connected to the Internet.

Darshu logged into her Hotmail account and spent the next hour sifting through a dozen friendly mails. *Send this to your 20 friends?* Delete.

She felt a bit puzzled as she opened a mail from a certain Pankaj. The sender was: Punk22@usa.net. His message was short:

> Hi,
> Read your story. It was nice. If your e-mail ever gets hacked, I'll let you know.
> Pankaj

Darshu felt a sudden terror. She had no idea how Pankaj – if it was really him – came to know of her *personal* e-mail

ID. *What is he trying to tell me through this message? Is he trying to suggest my e-mail can get hacked? Has it been hacked into already?* She straightened up and logged out immediately.

After about an hour, there was a knock on the door. Ritika was back.

'You won't believe what just happened. I received an e-mail from this guy called Pankaj,' said Darshu breathlessly.

'Now, who is Pankaj?'

'The guy who was my source for the hacking story.' Darshu looked distraught. 'Remember?'

'Okay ...'

'He messaged me to say that if my account gets hacked, he will inform me. Or maybe he will hack my account and inform me. I don't know what he meant!'

Ritika's face was blank, as if she were unsure of what the excitement was all about. 'Someone messing with you?' she finally asked.

It was a Sunday, bright and sunny. Darshu walked out of her apartment up Marredpally Road to Rezimental Street. She was drawn to MNR Cyber Café out of curiosity. But the shutters were still down when she reached the place.

She headed straight to the quaint little bakery in front of MNR. An old man, who looked like the same person from her previous visit, approached her with a glass of water that seemed muddied.

'I will take mineral water,' she said.

'Anything else?' asked the old man.

'Can I get a strong, hot cup of tea? Like you made last time?'

'Anything else?'

'What all do you prepare at this early hour?'

'Everything that you see on the menu.' The old man waited for her order.

She studied the menu. 'No, that's about it,' she said, handing the menu to him back. 'Do you know when this shop will open?' She pointed to the MNR Cyber Café.

'It usually opens at 8.30. But on Sunday, it will open around 10.30.'

'How long have they been in business? Are they new?'

'No, they've been here for more than three years. Maybe more.' He looked on at the shop and couldn't seem to recall exactly how long it had been around.

'Whose shop is it? Is it rented?'

'This was originally a fruit shop. When that closed, these college students started running their computer business here.' He shrugged, as if to say he didn't understand what their business entailed.

'There are two owners, right? They must be making lots of money?'

'Yeah, sometimes there is a rush. You know, college season. Sometimes even a fly refuses to enter the shop.'

She studied the signboard with an advertisement for a mobile operator. A small inscription at the edge mentioned the shop's name. *They truly are small-time shopkeepers!*

She finished her tea, paid her bill and sat there staring at her mobile uncertainly while the cyber café remained closed.

The colourful light from the computer screen flickered on Darshu's clothing. This was not her usual white-text-over-black-screen display. She was sitting in a special cubicle in the newsroom that was connected to the Internet.

She finished doing the first task she had set for herself. She changed her password into a new alphanumeric one. She deleted all the personal contacts stored in her e-mail account. She also removed her profile picture. Later, she did the same thing on Ryze social networking site, just to be sure that everything remained safe. She searched for a piece of paper before dialling Ritika's number from the office landline.

'Ritika, this is Darshu. Do you have Kanu's number?'

'What are you doing in the office on a Sunday?' came the reply from the other end.

'I came here to delete my account.'

'You what?'

'My e-mail got hacked.'

'You are sounding like an idiot. Someone sent you an e-mail, right? It's just an e-mail, right?'

'Yeah, I know. That's why I need Kanu's number.'

'He's coming this afternoon. He said he is busy now!'

'He's coming? Ritika, have you two started *dating*?'

'No. What's wrong with you? The system broke down. I paid 400 rupees,' Ritika clarified.

'Okay, fine.' Darshu breathed a sigh of relief.

Kanu was already there when Darshu reached home. He was wearing a jacket over T-shirt and jeans. An Afghani scarf was wrapped around his neck for extra protection from the dust. He was sitting on the floor with his unique *phone-attached-to-amplifier-attached-to-computer* device. Darshu was not surprised that the jugaad did not last too long. *Yeah, he calls it a modem. And it is broken!*

Kanu greeted Darshu with a couple of questions. 'You wanted my phone number? Something wrong?'

'Nothing. My e-mail. You know, Pankaj sent me a message saying that if someone hacks into my e-mail, he will inform me. First of all, I didn't give him my personal e-mail. *How did he get it?* Second, how will *he* know if my account gets hacked? That's scary, isn't it?'

Kanu turned to Ritika. 'Is she *always* like this?'

Darshu was not finished yet. 'Now, tell me, my closest friends keep sending me photos. I sent back photos to my friends. That's not safe. *Is it?*'

'I agree. That's not safe,' Kanu said. He turned his attention to Ritika again. 'You know, I was talking about this WLL network. Not many people know that this device can be condensed into a small chip which will directly connect the user to the Internet.' Kanu continued talking about computers and programming that made no sense.

Darshu threw her hands in the air and went inside. Ritika also went into the kitchen while Kanu continued with the work.

'Gosh, this is way too messy!' he cursed before getting up and dusting his hands as he tried to tuck the CPU back into the cabinet. 'Do you have a piece of cloth or something for dusting?' he called out.

Darshu threw a piece of silk cloth in his direction. It was Ritika's spaghetti strap top, as Ritika came out with a tissue box in her hand.

'Darshu, why did you give him my new spaghetti?' she screamed.

Kanu looked perplexed. 'You call this spaghetti? I thought spaghetti was some Italian food!'

'There are many things you don't know then, mister,' Darshu said teasingly. She then turned to Ritika. 'Rits, I've told you many times before, don't leave your clothes in my room.'

'Please, don't use that. Take this!' pleaded Ritika, as she gently pulled her spaghetti top out of Kanu's hands.

'That's okay. You girls can do the cleaning part. My work is done here. The system is working.' Kanu worked his hand into his jeans pocket and withdrew the key to his bike. 'Got to go,' he said.

'Where are you going? I was about to order biryani from Alps. You can have some biryani with us!'

'*Alps*? I thought you girls cook.'

'No, we never do the cooking part,' informed Ritika.

'Wait, you girls don't cook? I can show you a place that's the *best of the best*.'

The girls looked at each other.

Darshu, Ritika and Kanu sat inside Uncle's Kitchen food canteen with steaming parathas on their plates. It was a small joint, a little further away from Somajiguda Street. The newly-built flyover with a no-entry barrier from the left side had made access to the eatery even more obscure. Yet its patrons, mostly college students, never deserted this place.

'I told you, this place is *superlicious*!' exclaimed Kanu.

'They have six different kinds of parathas! And I can't finish my second,' Darshu added.

'I am surprised no one told you about this place!' Kanu said.

Kanu was sharing a portion of garlic paratha with Darshu, who was having the seasonal methi paratha. The onion paratha was yet to be served. For the first time in five days, Darshu was feeling comfortable in Kanu's presence. She had found out that he too was vegetarian like her, and both of them shared the same interests in music and movies.

Ritika, on the other hand, was tearing apart a poor bird with her teeth.

'This chicken masala tastes so amazing!' she said, licking her fingers.

So far, Ritika had been closer to Kanu. Now she appeared to him like a flesh-eating predator. *A murderer.*

Darshu and Kanu stole a glance at each other and winced. *Food does bring people together*, she thought.

The ride back home was tumultuous, especially for Kanu, what with a beautiful girl on each side. There was some confusion about who would enter the auto rickshaw after Darshu, but the relentless traffic did not allow them to debate the possibilities in detail. Ritika went in last.

The back seat was crowded but nobody complained.

When they reached Marredpally, close to the girls' home, Kanu was eager to pay for the ride. But Darshu intervened.

'I'll pay. Here, 40 rupees.' She pulled out the notes.

Kanu did not look happy. 'Spare me! You paid for the food as well.'

'Some other day!' Darshu smiled.

The auto was gone. Kanu searched for his keys and pulled them out from his jeans pocket.

'Oh, I forgot my Afghani scarf,' he said.

'Leave it for us. We will use it for dusting,' Darshu said smiling.

'I did not even check if the modem is working. I will come up and be gone in a minute.'

'We know it's working. After all, you've worked on it,' replied Darshu.

'You want me to go?'

'Yes,' Darshu smiled.

Ritika was feeling tired. She said goodbye and went inside, leaving Kanu and Darshu behind.

'I must say thanks. I never get an opportunity to get out of my cubicle,' Kanu said, as he got on his bike and prepared to kick-start it.

'Likewise. We wouldn't have known about this place. Thank you!'

Kanu got his old bike going, a few sidelights dangling from wires, stole one more glance at her and then he was gone.

That evening, Darshu decided to go to the cyber café again. She told herself the reasons behind this visit: return the Afghani scarf, and her Hotmail account. However, when she reached the café, she had changed her mind.

'I didn't have any work and was alone, so I came. To browse,' she said, returning the scarf to Kanu.

Darshu was being honest. She found his company surprisingly relaxing. She was hardly ever drawn to strangers. They had first met for the purpose of a news story. This was their sixth encounter, and here she was!

'What about Ritika? Where is she?' Kanu asked.

'She has this rocking group of office friends ... in Banjara.'

'You didn't join them?'

'I did join them once. But you know how it is. It really gets weird listening to drunken people. After a while, you curse yourself for going to the party!'

'Hmm, but the cabins are all packed.'

'Not a problem. I can wait!'

'You can use my system, if you want.'

'No, I'll wait.'

'Have a seat then.' Kanu gestured to the visitor's chair and sat next to her.

While Bansi worked at the machine on the counter, keying away college reports, Darshu and Kanu discussed the e-mail sent by Pankaj.

'I don't know why Pankaj would send it. His message was weird. I don't know what to do. Should I forward the mail to your account?'

'That's not needed. The truth is he has this thing for girls' e-mail accounts. I think you must be his new victim.'

'Really?' Darshu was alarmed. 'What do I do now?'

'Nothing.'

'What? Why?'

'Any change you make will be sent out to your backup e-mail ID. I think you must be using the same password for every other account.'

'How do you know?'

'Well, everyone makes the same mistake. The only practical solution is to save contact addresses, maybe write them down on a paper, and discard the account.'

'Damn!'

'Or else, you can share your password with me. I will keep it safe!'

'You are kidding, right?'

'You think so?'

'You are kidding, right?' she repeated.

'Okay, here's another solution. You can try this two-step authentication set-up. When you log in with your new password, it will ask for a second level passcode, which you'll receive on your phone. Now that can make your account more secure ... Unless someone has already cloned your mobile number.'

'Cloned what?'

'Cloned your mobile number.'

'Why would anyone clone my mobile number?'

'For the same reason someone would hack your e-mail account.'

'So what should I do?'

'I told you, give me your password. I will keep it safe.'

'You are kidding, right?'

Kanu smiled.

The next day, she ran into Kanu at the Secunderabad branch of Oriental Bank. The place was a walk away from her office. She spotted him in a queue to deposit money.

'Is that black money you are holding in that bundle?' she teased.

'That's correct! How did you know?'

'I know instinctively when things are illegal.'

'Ah, like that!'

'Yes, like that.'

She got a token from the next counter, for which there was a long wait, then took a seat in the waiting area.

After he had finished, Kanu walked up to her and whispered, 'It's a very long queue for depositing a demand draft. Do you want me to hack the queue?'

'Really? How will you do that?'

'Let me see.' Kanu put his hands into his trouser pockets, as if searching for something. 'I thought I had the bank manager in my pocket. Where did he slip away?' he said, blinking sheepishly.

'Thanks for your effort. I will manage.' Darshu smacked his arm mockingly.

'You know, sometimes having a good contact helps. Take my example. People don't value my worth. But, you know, a time will come when people will salute me for having done the right thing.'

Kanu took the seat next to hers and continued explaining his virtues. The wait was long and Kanu was pleasant company, always ready with his expert opinion on everything. They discussed PayPal and online transactions while waiting for her turn to deposit money for her online course. Kanu wasn't convinced about the online examination format.

'But you can cheat in an online exam, right?'

'No, you can't!'

'But while you are in front of your computer, they are in, let's say, some place in Germany, you can open a book and write. How will they know?'

'They assign a computer institute where they will have their dedicated computers. Exams will be conducted online.'

'Okay, I get it. But still, the screen can be shared. Right?'

'I don't know about that. But it's a language course. Why would anyone want to cheat?'

'Language? Okay, what about the keyboard?'

'It's French. Same keyboard.'

'Last I remember, you said you are learning German?'

'I am learning German. The exam is for French language.'

'How many languages do you know?'

'Five. Maybe six.'

'I know six languages as well. Telugu. English. Hindi. And my computer languages include Cobol, C++ and JAVA.'

'Yeah, add body language to the list. That will make it seven.'

'Good idea!'

After submitting her form, they spent most of the day together, eating lunch, watching an inter-school cricket match at St Patrick's School, visiting St Mary's Church and finally, went to meet Ritika outside her office.

Darshu enjoyed the time they spent. She felt they had a connection, some kind of bond, and the conversation between them was easy and unforced, as if they had known each other for a long time.

When Ritika walked out, she was surprised to see Darshu and Kanu waiting for her.

'You guys called me almost two hours back. You've been waiting since then? You guys have *no* work or what?' Ritika asked.

'You know me. I am a journalist,' replied Darshu.

'Should have told me you were waiting. I could have come out earlier,' Ritika said.

'I wanted to show him our office. Why don't you come along? The other day, you wanted to meet Ayesha.'

'Ayesha, yes. Just for PR! But not today.'

'Why not?'

'I am not prepared. I will join you some other time.' With that, Ritika left with a few of her colleagues.

Darshu and Kanu walked to the *Deccan Courier* building, which was not far away from ITCC. The office wasn't fancy. A big room was divided up with glass partitions into editorial and marketing divisions.

They sat in the visitors' room and she began to explain to Kanu the process of newsgathering, filing reports and page-making.

Kanu liked her, more so when she tried explaining things that were stupid and uninteresting. *Why don't they switch to desktop publishing?* he wondered. 'Is that your number?' he asked, looking at the notice board that had a list of reporters' names and numbers pinned to it. 'What kind of number is that, ending with 6969?'

Darshu did not say anything for a while. Then she smiled. 'I thought it was easy to remember.'

Later, just before reaching home, Darshu checked her mobile. She had a text message from Kanu: *rchd home*?

She smiled and replied: *not yet*.

After about five minutes, she got another message: *n now?*

Darshu had never been much into texting. She preferred phone calls. It was easier to have a clear conversation that way instead of messaging back and forth. But this was a slightly more complicated situation. So she messaged back: *why u don't have any work or what?*

She did not get any reply until eleven that night: *thx for reminding abt work. got it done. no work now ;)*

They continued exchanging texts until he asked her to come online for a Yahoo! Chat. He gave away his avatar: DIGITAL_GOD. Darshu added his ID to her messenger and pinged him:

11.41 p.m.

DARSHU: hey, wassup Digital God

DIGITAL_GOD: hi. nothing much. at home and u?

DARSHU: hahhaha .... No ... at this time i m in my office! damn!

DIGITAL_GOD: good for u ... you got to report so many things ... we are ... *ahem* ... criminals. no work. so always at home

DARSHU: hahahaha ..... GYAN!

11.49 p.m.

DIGITAL_GOD: anything new happening?

DARSHU: was thinking of going home this Wednesday

... christmas holiday

DIGITAL_GOD: where is ur home?

DARSHU: dehradun

DIGITAL_GOD: wow ... it must be cold there ...

DARSHU: yup bus ghar jaooo khayo piyo so jaooo yeh hi plan tha but no leave :(

DIGITAL_GOD: know what. i like that concept ... hunt ... for food ... sleep till you feel hungry again. repeat

DARSHU: hahhahahhaha i like the *repeat* part

11.57 p.m.

DIGITAL_GOD: so what r u doin tmrw?

DARSHU: don't know. hav to attend 1 conference

DIGITAL_GOD: wher is tht conference

DARSHU: kakatiya. i will call u if i m close to ur area its getting late. 12 already

DIGITAL_GOD: ya, time for me to start working

DARSHU: gud. ur office time begins now ... *ahem* ... criminals after all. hahaha

00:02 a.m.

DIGITAL_GOD: chalo gudnite :)

DARSHU: gn. sweet dreams :)

Darshu logged out.

The next day Darshu was tasked with the additional responsibility of visiting a school function at R.P. Road before covering the Kakatia conference. Obviously, she was not very happy with the arrangement. By the time she finished her day's work, it was already seven in the evening. She thought of calling Kanu, but instead took an auto rickshaw home. At 7.40 p.m., she got a text message from him asking her to get ready for a paav-bhaji session.

rchng ur place in 15 min. hittin u wth paav bhaji today!

She messaged back: *whr s this paav baji place agn?*

He replied: *u ll know*

Darshu had been single for as long as she'd been in Hyderabad. It was not as if she was never approached by guys. On the contrary, she was besieged with inane requests: Can I get your phone number? What's your Yahoo! ID? Where do you live? Can I book you for a movie tonight? Can I walk you home? Are you free this evening? You are very pretty. Has anyone ever told you that?

The ones who expressed a romantic interest did not appeal to her. And the ones she flirted with – made eye contact and smiled at – never seemed to respond.

All that was about to change. Get ready for a late-night paav-bhaji date? Why not!

Kanu arrived outside Darshu's flat early and called her. She did not answer. He tried again, impatient, but disconnected when he saw her walk towards him. She smiled and flashed her phone at him: *Hacker ... calling*, the screen said.

'For God's sake! I have a name!' said Kanu, trying to snatch at the handset.

'Bad manners!' Darshu said, and slipped it into her purse. 'Very bad manners to snatch things from a girl!'

Kanu kick-started the bike, put it into gear and waited for her to hop on. 'I have a name. And it's a really simple one,' he said.

'I know, Kanu,' she whispered. 'By the way, what kind of name is that? *Kanu*?'

Kanu accelerated as he hit the main road. 'My mom used to call me Kanu –'

The wind and the traffic drowned his voice and Darshu couldn't hear the rest.

She felt heady with the excitement of riding pillion. She could feel her heart beat faster as she pressed her body against him for support and gripped his shoulders. But before long, he had stopped in front of the food court on Necklace Road on the banks of Hussain Sagar in the heart of the city.

He put his bike on its stand and gestured to the food joint.

'Paav-bhaji paradise.'

'This is Necklace Road. I have been here many times before,' she said.

'There, that shop you see. They will serve me *free* food if you want.'

'Really? Is he is your uncle, that old man? You must be coming here often then?'

'Nah, he's an old client. I wrote an article for them. Come here often? No, that fellow will pester me to hell. That's the reason I don't come here at all.'

'Oh, *like that*.'

'Yeah, like that.'

'If I were you, I would come here every day. Free food!'

They carried on their small talk, debating the merits and demerits of a free lunch, but the place was packed. Far from the sitting areas, they found a wooden bench for visitors that not many knew about.

'Killer lake view, isn't it?' he said.

'Yeah!'

'See there, Lord Buddha is blessing the tourists only after they've left,' he said, pointing to a boat sailing by a gigantic statue of the Buddha. 'Which means he does not like to be disturbed by tourists!'

'That's not a tourist boat. That's some promotional thing. I think they are planning to put up a show or something.'

'If you are thinking I set this up for you, you may be right!'

'Shut up!'

'You shut up!'

'Shut up!'

'You shut up!'

The troupe on the boat started performing, just in time to distract them from their fight.

They sat there in that near-isolated area for about twenty minutes, admiring the view and the performance.

By that time, there was a free table at the joint and they eagerly went ahead and claimed it.

On their second date, they went to a dhaba on the outskirts of the city, where they were served steaming jowar roti with chilli chutney. Darshu was happy to note that Kanu shared her culinary tastes completely. They laughed over their mutual obsession with melodramatic Hindi films, and he promised to share his movie collection with her.

But instead, he took her to a movie on their next date. And they argued over the climax of the plot and how far-fetched it seemed. The argument began at a dine-in restaurant and continued till the time Kanu had dropped her to her apartment. Yet, it remained unfinished. After he'd left, he texted: *OK, u win d Christmas treat.*

On their next date they went go-karting at Kompally. Kanu had lived in the Kompally neighbourhood before moving to Secunderabad. Almost everyone at the go-karting circuit recognized him instantly and took a keen interest in Darshu. She had never been behind the wheel of a go-kart. Now, all of a sudden, she was in the driver's seat.

He held her hand to calm her as she nervously attended to the instructions of the guide. He leaned in and sneaked a kiss on her cheek to reassure her. She smiled and raced ahead as he stepped back away from the vehicle.

She could feel his moist lips long after she had crossed the finishing line.

Later, as they hung out together in the track field, talking about movies, music and books, two SISI men kept a close watch on them. It was their job to keep track of Kanu, who was on their watch list. While Kanu and Darshu walked the circuit, stopping at the souvenir shops on the side paths, the men followed them at a distance.

The couple remained seated on the bench, near the finishing line, long after the sun had set. They almost looked like teenagers who had lied to their parents to be there, doing things that they shouldn't.

From a distance, the SISI men saw them kissing. At this point, they decided that the best thing for them to do would be to leave the lovebirds alone!

FIVE

20–23 December 2006

In the conference room on the fifth floor of the *Deccan Courier* office, Gaurav Rathod wrote four distinct words on a whiteboard: *Increase Revenue and Readership*. The only other person present was Ayesha Pathan. Normally, Ayesha would just shut up and bear the insufferable presentation. But on this day, she had been summoned for a special assignment.

'Why do you want me to cover this story on Sathyamev? If it's a negative story you want, why don't you ask Darshu to do it?' Ayesha said.

'No, not negative. I said, critical. And we are not going to publish the story either. We only show them we have all the necessary information to do such a story. Consider this: Sathyamev promised to double their ad spending in our publication if we don't run a critical story about it. Imagine what would happen if we start digging out all the murky details. I have prepared a note on Rana Rajput using all my contacts. I want you to read it.'

Ayesha took the piece of paper he held out.

Rana Rajput was born in Hyderabad forty-nine years ago. His father, Agra Narayan Rajput, was a rich farmer who owned massive swathes of farmland in and around the city of Hyderabad.

From his youth, Rana's dream was to develop an integrated township project on a family-held twenty-acre plot in Hyderabad. But, sensing Rana's disruptive, unusual plan, Agra Narayan forced his son to pursue a management course overseas.

Two years later in 1977, Rana returned to India with an MBA degree from Ohio University. With an international degree under his belt, he hit the ground running, launching the Dhananjay Heritage Hotel by converting an old colonial building, owned by the family, into a twenty-two-room boutique hotel. Unfortunately, his venture turned sour within six months, and he was forced to sell the property to pay off depositors.

But in 1982, luck smiled on him in the form of Andhra Pradesh's new industrial policy. The newly formed Andhra Pradesh Urban Industrial Development Corporation (APUIDC) invited bids for a state-sponsored assistance programme to create a robust manufacturing-based economy in Indian cities.

Rana, with the help of his contacts in government offices, obtained a subsidy of fifty lakh rupees from APUIDC for his Shrishasatyam Spinning Mills –

Employment for City Youth (SSM-ECY) initiative. As per the terms of the agreement, within one year SSM-ECY had to set up a massive yarn mill on the family land that could employ hundreds of local workers.

In reality, the reported factory was nothing more than an iron structure, with machines that were either obsolete or in a non-working condition. On completion of the project, SSM-ECY started making low-quality yarn that had no market.

Rana bribed auditors to validate the project and write a favourable completion report.

Three months from the day the assets were transferred to Rana, SSM-ECY was closed down, reportedly due to a 'massive fire in the factory'. The factory remained closed and the machines were either sold off or returned to the original manufacturers.

Rana benefited from this 'deal' tremendously. Instead of paying a high interest rate on the money he had borrowed from a private bank, he was sitting on a big pile of cash procured through subsidy. Rana invested a part of his gain to purchase more land and set up subsidiaries under the SSM brand.

'But what about Sathyamev?' Ayesha said, puzzled.

'That again is not Rana's creation. Here, read this.' Gaurav passed on another note.

Computer programming in the 80s was a hotbed of nerds. The idea behind many IT start-ups was to offer low-cost solutions to the clients in Western countries. Sathyamev was among the first Indian companies to recognize the potential of the highly skilled, educated and cheap Indian workforce. But between 1987, when the company was founded, and 2000, when Y2K hit the scene, Sathyamev saw several change of guards. In 1992, when the company went public, it was reported that Vasu Kumar, who was one of the founders of the company, had a falling out with Rana. The conflict ended in the two co-founders parting ways. Vasu had to quit Sathyamev and face a three-year ban on starting another IT company of his own.

Following Vasu's exit, Rana solidified his leadership position within Sathyamev's management structure. Then, in May 2001, Sathyamev's American Depository Receipt (ADR) was listed on the New York Stock Exchange, raising 140.8 million dollars or about 753 crore rupees. He channelled part of this money into a more complex investment deal with his Mauritius subsidiary by exploiting international mismatches that allowed companies to make investment and avoid taxes. He also structured the operations in Mauritius in such a way that investments and profits from the US and other countries flowed into Mauritius.

'You know so much about Rana. Why don't you do the story yourself?' Ayesha asked.

'The story may not be entirely true – it's based on what people I know closely told me about Rana. Read that last line about the Mauritius subsidiary. Well, nobody knows what the Mauritius subsidiary actually does, but many believed that money might have found its way back into India through the back-channel hawala route.'

'Wow! But why don't we report such stories?'

'We don't know if it's true. Even if it is, why not monetize it?'

Ayesha looked at him, stunned. She had no further questions.

The following day, Ayesha sat beside Samba Rajput in Sathyamev's nineteenth-floor conference room under the glow of Rana Rajput's face, beamed live on a projected screen. Rana's image seemed like a million tiny lamps of different colours lit all at once.

'Are there any questions, Ayesha?' Rana asked.

Ayesha lowered her eyes to the piece of paper in front of her, then looked back at the screen. 'No, I think I'm done.'

'I have spoken to Gaurav. I know he will guide you. Thanks for coming!' Rana smiled.

Ayesha collected her notepad and left the room.

As the door slid shut again, Samba leaned forward to speak to Rana.

'From the report the SISI men submitted, I can tell he is Kanha. These days he has changed his name to Kanu.'

'How can you be so sure, Samba?'

'The SISI team tracked every detail. They visited every place he had lived in. I'm confident he is the one.'

'So what's your plan?' asked Rana.

'I don't know.' Samba stared anxiously at the large screen.

'Are you planning to give him some kind of protection? Or are you waiting to reward him for stealing our data? Take my advice. Don't try to protect this kid – he'll always remain a threat to us.'

Rana's voice was shaky, as was his image. The network that projected him was getting disrupted. The sight was as dreadful as it was alarming. Then the connection snapped.

Kanu followed his usual route to his home in Secunderabad. As he put his Yamaha on its stand and walked out of the parking lot, he noticed two shiny black Mercedes parked in front of his door, along with the two guards staring at him.

As he drew closer, he saw one guard lean towards a partially open car window. He could see the silhouette of a man inside, but couldn't make out his features.

The security guard stepped back and an elderly man emerged from the car. He was thin, dressed in a black suit and leaning on a black cane.

Is that Nanu? Kanu wondered. The creases had grown deeper and the old man little resembled the grandpa he remembered playing with on his way home from school. Kanu's grandfather, Agra Narayan Rajput, had been his constant companion along the busy streets of Hyderabad.

Kanu walked toward his grandpa and leaned forward to touch his feet.

Just then, another man stepped out of the back door of the second Mercedes. Samba Uncle? Kanu drew a sharp breath.

'Kanha, or Kanu, what should I call you?' Samba said with a slight grin. 'Hmm ... so, this is where you live. Won't you invite us in?'

Kanu stared at his uncle silently for what seemed like a long time. The name Kanha brought back memories he wished to forget. He could feel his heart pulsating.

Agra Narayan walked towards his grandson. 'It's good to know you've chosen computer programming as your profession, just like your dad,' said the old man. 'I'm sure you must be surprised to see us all here at this hour –'

Samba did not wait for his father to finish. 'How long do you think you can remain in hiding, Kanha? Have you ever thought of your mom? She's not keeping well ... but what do you care?'

'I know what I'm doing,' Kanu said, turning away from the visitors.

The old man began again. 'That's okay. We've come here to talk to you. It's our duty to guide you. C'mon, let's go inside. Let's see where you live.'

The passageway where Kanu parked his Yamaha led to his house on the ground floor. It was an old construction, with cobwebs hanging from the ceiling and walls and dust all over the floor.

Kanu unlocked the door and showed the visitors into his living room, which was devoid of any family photographs or souvenirs. He pulled out the easy chair from behind the computer desk and offered it to his grandpa. 'Sorry, I don't have enough chairs. But you can sit on my beanbag, if that's okay?' he said to his uncle.

'Not a problem. We are fine,' Samba said.

The old man let go of his cane and cautiously sat on the chair. Samba stood near the computer table at a comfortable distance from the others.

'I'm told you run a pay-per-visit Internet café? That's good. We also had chains of *i-café*, you know, providing cheap Internet access and stuff. It was a franchisee model. If you must know, it didn't work out the way we planned.' Samba's voice was cold and flat. 'We did a background check on you. Seems your Internet business is doing well. What's your main source of income? Hacking?'

Kanu remained silent.

The old man studied Kanu's eyes, wondering why Samba would raise such a topic. 'Samba, you requested me to come so that I could talk to Kanha,' said Agra Narayan. 'Will you allow me?'

Samba made a dismissive gesture with his hand. 'Fine, you speak.'

'It's been nine years since you left home. We did everything possible to find you. I know you wrote letters to your mom. But that's not all. You must also be with your mom and your ailing father –' said the old man.

'Why have you come here?' Kanu asked, raising his voice. 'What's wrong with you all?'

'I know you hated us when you left. Now there's no point in being a rebel. Look what you've done. You've started disrupting the lives of others,' continued the old man.

'Nanu, I know well what you mean, but there's no point talking about this *now*.'

Samba intervened. 'Think of your mom. She is my sister. Think about your dad.'

'You snatched away his hard-earned work, leaving him on a wheelchair to lead the life of a dead man. How can I *not* think of him?'

'We never wanted to hurt …' said Samba.

'You must let go of all things past. I know you must have your reasons not to believe us. But Rana is not a bad person at heart. He still loves your mom more than anyone else in the world … Those were the dark days,' said the old man.

Samba was getting impatient. 'You must get past your feelings. They're no good … not for you or the family. Even Rana bhai is willing to forgive you. I've a message from him …'

Samba gestured for his security guard to hand over the laptop. As he clicked on the media player, Rana's face appeared on the screen. *Kanha, it's good to know you live in our city, you wretched little kid. You left my sister crying. Now, come back, and I'll give you a nice job –*

Samba clicked the pause button. 'There's more in the message, but I won't play it. His messages can be scary at times. I don't want you to think we don't care.' He turned to his father. 'If you have anything more to add, tell him now. I'm done.'

As Samba left the room, Agra Narayan looked at his grandson expectantly. Even under the harsh rebelliousness, the old man could see the same, loving grandson he had known.

'There's no denying that you are immensely gifted, but you must be careful. Your dad was just as talented. But talent alone cannot be enough. You have to be stronger,' said the old man as he walked towards the door. 'I feel sorry I cannot offer anything more. But you be strong and do what you must.' With that, he walked away.

Kanu stood near the door, lost in his thoughts long after the Mercedes was gone. *'Your dad was just as talented,'* echoed in his head as he stumbled on to his beanbag.

The hardest thing for him was to confront his past, his fears of not being strong enough, of not being listened to. He picked up his laptop and powered it on. The lifeless screen lit up and a sepia-coloured image of a young man in his mid-thirties, smiling, while working on the prized computer of the eighties – a monochrome monitor with a block-shaped mouse and a keyboard – appeared.

Kanu's father, Vasu Kumar, was a software programmer with a Master's degree in computer science from MIT. He was his teacher and guide. Even before Kanu started going to school, his father had taught him to power on computers and type passwords. 'Tell me the password,' Vasu would ask. 'V-A-S-U-ENTER,' the little kid would reply.

Little Kanu spent most of his time playing *Silpheed*. By the time he was six, his father had taught him to open files and perform basic computer operations, and he would often take Kanu to his office and let him play games on his computers.

Kanu's earliest memory of his dad teaching him computer games went back to an hour of playing shooting arrows to deflate balloons. 'You must shoot low and release it high to find your target,' Vasu would say. 'After all, what is an archer without his arrows?'

By the time Kanu was eight, he was working on an Intel 486 running on Windows 3.11 with DOS 4.0 at his father's workplace. While Kanu's adopted elder brother, Bala, was lucky to learn MS Paint, Kanu was busy learning diagnostic tools and updating drivers.

The first thing Kanu saw upon entering the passageway was a couple of thick glass doors separating him from the computer room. Behind the doors, his dad was being held against his will. Two men were trying to tie him down to a chair, rocking back and forth. Kanu's recollections were all fragmentary. *His tiny hands trying to open the door, he was screaming and running back to the room where he played computer games – his attempt to find something to break open the glass door, pulling out a keyboard from the monitor to do this, the monitor falling on him, blood splattering on the floor with the broken glass ...*

Kanu woke up in a sudden terror, uncertain where he was. Still crumpled on the beanbag, he looked for signs of morning behind the window curtain. It was still dark, a few minutes past midnight, and way past dinner time. He decided to step outside for some fresh air.

Kanu pulled out his Yamaha and raced toward the Secunderabad station. It was a cold December night, and he realized at once that he wasn't wearing enough clothes.

At the Railway Canteen, amidst a bustling crowd of harassed passengers, Kanu had to make an effort to sip hot tea from a paper cup. He was shivering. The masala dosa remained uneaten on his plate. Even among thousands of people, it was as if he sat alone, in a distant world of his own.

SIX

26 March–24 June 1992

In 1991, a new national economic policy liberalized trade regulations in services previously controlled by the government, and Sathyamev Computer Services was set to prosper in the new, liberal, international economy.

Like most start-ups, Sathyamev began small. But Vasu had a vision for the budding computer company. In less than five years, Sathyamev grew exponentially, competing with the likes of IBMM. It boasted five offices at different locations in Hyderabad, and the growing demand in global software development ensured that Sathyamev was on a path to becoming a major global player in the software industry.

The rapid growth of Sathyamev convinced Rana to move away from his spinning mill and real estate development business, and take an active interest in the day-to-day affairs of the company.

Though Vasu was never friends with Rana, the two were destined to collaborate and clash. In Sathyamev's formative years, Vasu wanted funds to expand his company's footprint, and Rana was the only willing investor. The two relatives (Vasu was married to Rana's cousin, Ketki) finally forged their professional alliance, and Rana came on board as a founding partner of Sathyamev. But five years later, Vasu's decision to accept Rana's money weighed on him heavily.

On 26 March 1992, Rana invited a team of financial professionals to Sathyamev's board meeting. He asked them to scrutinize the revenue figures, balance sheets, cash flow and investor details so that he could take the company public.

In the board meeting, Rana explained that listing the company with 'cumulative' revenue figures and launching a PR campaign would help them reap rich dividends. His pitch was to raise extra money from the capital market. 'The end result,' Rana declared, 'would make us all, including the new appointees, millionaires overnight.'

Vasu sat through the meeting without saying a word. He could sense his influence waning in the company he had founded. Earlier that day, he had rejected his brother-in-law's idea, but they seemed to have many fundamental disagreements, beyond the immediate matter of going public. His brother-in-law's proposed choice of the new board members, 'the new appointees', was unacceptable. The manipulation of workforce numbers made no sense to him. He also detested the new legal and financial team as well as the PR campaign.

Finally, he couldn't take it any more. 'I see so many loopholes in this proposal,' Vasu said. 'If the plan is to raise money for Sathyamev by falsifying figures, then I am not in it with you, Rana. We cannot be inducting a new team just for such selfish interests. This won't work in the long-term. To be honest, I can never be part of this plan,' Vasu said and abruptly ended the meeting.

But Rana was persistent. He realized he could not afford Vasu storming out. Later that day, he suggested a deal: if Vasu quit the company and relinquished control, Rana would give him 15 per cent equity shares. It was an agonizing choice for Vasu – he was being forced out of the company he had built from scratch.

In the following days, Vasu decided to involve his father-in-law, Agra Narayan, and other family elders to settle the dispute. But before they could hold a meeting, he contracted a sudden, inexplicable illness.

Three days after the board meeting, news came through that Vasu had been taken to the hospital after suffering from a sudden paralytic attack. Agra Narayan rushed to the ICU. The team of doctors said Vasu had suffered from conversion disorder, an unexplainable condition caused by sudden rage or distress.

'He is suffering from uncontrolled tremors, numbness and paralysis. There is no explanation or source for such a sudden and debilitating illness,' explained the head of the neuroscience division. 'In Vasu's case, it may have been caused by a devastating incident he recently experienced. His son's injury is the most likely explanation.'

Samba confirmed the doctor's hypothesis. 'On the day Vasu was admitted to the hospital, both he and Kanu were in the Sathyamev office. Kanu was playing computer games when suddenly the monitor fell on him. Vasu saw his son soaked in blood, buried under the weight of the device,' said Samba.

Rana's version was similar. 'We heard a noise and rushed into the room to see Kanu injured and Vasu suffering a panic attack. We tried to revive Vasu, bring him back to consciousness. The security team arrived at the scene and also tried to help Vasu. Instead of waiting for paramedics, we rushed them both to the ambulance, which had arrived downstairs,' he explained to his sister, Ketki.

Ketki believed everything Rana and the team of doctors said. But the attending nurse's verdict was the most difficult to bear: 'Unfortunately, the stroke has left your husband incapacitated. He cannot speak or live normally, and he has lost all bodily functions.'

In this sudden turn of events, Vasu was held captive in his hospital bed, and along with him, his wife Ketki too was caught up, nursing him. And thus, Rana got what he wanted – complete control over Sathyamev.

SEVEN

24–25 December 2006

It was Christmas Eve, but all Darshu could do was stare glumly at her phone. She was supposed to be out on a date with Kanu, but it had been more than two days since she had last seen him. Her three phone calls and five text messages had gone unanswered, and now she feared the worst.

Instead of calling him again, she took pre-emptive action. She began to make a mental list of the reasons why she shouldn't be bothered about what clearly appeared to be the sign of a break-up. Initially, she had thought Kanu had just been busy with work. Of late, she'd had more worrying thoughts: *Is he busy with some college girl in his cyber café? Why is he unavailable? Why?*

His unresponsiveness only made her want him more.

She looked at her phone again. Memories of better times overpowered her as she collapsed on to her bed and fell asleep.

The next morning, Darshu didn't bother to wait for a call. Instead, she went straight to MNR Cyber Café. The shop had its shutters down. 'Is he playing the hard-to-get game?' she thought.

Darshu felt tears sting her eyes, but she refused to believe it was all over. She called Ritika and they decided to meet at Kamat Restaurant in Secunderabad.

Slouching on a sofa at the restaurant, Darshu held a glass of sweet lime juice in her hand. She was staring off into the distance, seemingly uninterested in the conversation. Ritika sat opposite her, stirring her coffee and looking around for people she knew.

'I'd definitely not hurt anyone like this. You know, among my few dates, there was this boring PhD student who took me out to dinner, picked me up from college, took me to a temple – made me feel almost like his sister! But I was so caring. You know,' said Ritika, 'I took him to the gaming zone, ordered a pizza and told him he was more like a brother to me!'

'At least he could have called me ...'

'Yeah, this sucks!'

'I think he is playing a hard-to-get dude. I read it in *Cosmo*. At first he is caring. And then next thing you know, he's gone. I almost fell for this guy. I feel so stupid.'

'Yeah, on a day like this.'

'I went to his shop twice. Even that poor guy Bansi doesn't know anything. I feel so stupid!'

'Don't worry, it's a phase.'

'I think I'll have some vodka.'

'Now?'

'At the party. Can I join you?'

'But you don't like our parties.'

'I know. I'm just saying – never mind. You're right. I don't enjoy the company of your office friends.'

'Seriously, but you're most welcome to come join us. Know what? You *must* come to the party and –'

'Nah, I'll just go watch TV. That's what I do every Christmas.'

'Poor thing! This is why I'll never leave Ritwik.'

'Yeah, don't ever do that. Your names also match.'

That evening Darshu was sprawled out on the couch, watching her favourite programme, *Bollywood Biggies*, when her cellphone lit up: *Sorry I cud nt reply. Can u meet me pls? I am at ISKON mandir.*

Kanu was listed as 'Hacker' on her cellphone. She re-read the message and looked up at the ceiling aimlessly. Three days of no reply and now this? Why did he write PLEASE?

She messaged back: 'k.'

The Hare Rama Hare Krishna temple was not far from her place. As she walked down the street, her yellow-green salwar-kameez made her skin glow in the dingy streetlight.

Darshu walked into the temple and folded her hands, palms together. *Make me successful*, she prayed. She surveyed the length of the temple, searching.

Kanu wasn't there.

She decided to look for him outside. Far away, she glimpsed him sitting on a bench all by himself. She wanted to go at once and meet him but decided to stand among the waiting devotees to accept prasadam.

How well Darshu remembered the first time she had seen Kanu. He had been holding a cable in one hand and a toner in another, that eternally cheerful smile pasted across his face. She liked his attitude towards the students, always ready to take on any challenge. But on this day, he sat in a corner, looking desolate. He had wrapped himself in a dusty shawl and was shivering from the cold.

'Hi! Are you okay?' she asked.

He looked at her, stunned, as if he had lost his voice. She knew at once something was wrong. With the back of her hand, she felt his temple.

'You're burning up! You have a fever. What are you doing here?'

'Nah, it's nothing.'

'Here, prasadam.' She offered him part of the khichiri and ate the rest of it. 'You should have told me you weren't well.'

'I promised I'd take you somewhere on Christmas.'

'No, let me take you to a hospital.' She held his arm tightly, forcing him to stand. 'You need medical care.'

'I am fine. I am fine –' He sat back again. 'It's just – I can't feel anything – I've been unsure of what to do.' His voice began to choke as he spoke. 'I don't know what I am doing.' A crease formed between his brows. He swallowed and glanced down at his hands. He bowed his head, fighting back tears.

'What happened? Is something wrong?' She sat alongside him. 'It's okay. Tell me what happened.'

'I don't know if I should tell you –'

She knew something was wrong. Did someone commit suicide? She had experienced the suicide of a family member and she had acted at the time much like Kanu. 'Kanu, what happened?'

'That story you wrote in the *Deccan Courier* ... and then they forced you to issue a clarification on Sathyamev? Do you know who those people are? Whose company it is?'

'No.'

'That's the company my father built.'

'*Sathyamev*?' she gasped. 'Really? Rana Rajput is your fa ...'

'No, he is my uncle. My father, Vasu Kumar, built that computer firm. I remember those early days when he worked night and day. I used to visit him in his small office. We were very ordinary people ... a very middle class family ... my father, my mom and me. My father was a programmer. He built the company and my uncle snatched it away. They put him in a wheelchair – imprisoned him for life.'

'No way!'

'They came to my home two days ago. They said they'll do to me what they did to my father.'

Darshu had no words to console him. 'You're shivering.' She wrapped her arm around his shoulders, pulling him protectively against her body. She thought for a moment and stood up. 'Wait, I'll bring a blanket from the temple.'

'I am fine, you don't ne –'

But before Kanu could finish Darshu was on her way towards the temple. She came back with a coarse blanket and draped it around his shoulders.

'Don't worry, you will be fine,' she assured him.

'Thanks for coming.'

'Shh ... you just stay calm. I know how you feel.'

'I was a little boy ... I couldn't stop what was happening to my father. There were two doors separating us. I could see them – my uncle – through the glass door, but I couldn't open it!' His brow furrowed, his fists clenched.

'You were in school ...'

'I was eight. I was studying in class three,' Kanu said as a tear rolled down his cheek. 'I used to go to his office to play games. There was this red-carpeted computer room where my dad used to work. He left me there with the computer. He must have gone to a meeting or something, but he didn't come back. The second the game was over, I started looking around for him in the other rooms. There was no one in the building. Then I saw my uncle walking back and forth in the corridor. My father was in the other room. Two doors separated us –'

She moved a little closer and held him tight, as if to say: 'You can let it go.' But she did not interrupt.

'At first, it seemed like my uncle was having an argument with my father. Then I saw him pushing my father and tying him to a chair. I saw my father being tied … it must have been painful … I saw my dad throw up … I think he called for help. Finally, he fell asleep.'

Shivers ran through Kanu's body as he continued. 'The door was locked. I tried hard, but couldn't get through. I started calling for help, but no one came. I went back to my room to find something I could use to break open the door. I tried pulling a keyboard. It was then I think that the monitor fell on me … I don't know what happened next. When I regained consciousness …' His voice broke, and he could not continue.

Darshu stared at him wordlessly. Kanu looked into the distance.

'My dad was lying in the hospital, awake but lifeless. He would never walk again. Or talk …'

The blanket was falling off. She took one end of it and wrapped herself with it and held him tight.

'I told my mom. I told my Nanu. No one believed me. My mom believed her brothers. There was only one person who wanted to help me – my brother, Bala. But he was far away, at a boarding school.' He paused for breath.

'Eventually, I couldn't take it any longer,' Kanu continued. 'Watching my dad being dragged in a wheelchair … It was painful. He couldn't move without assistance. Looking at people expectantly was all he could manage. So I ran away … no one knew except for my Nanu. I stayed with our driver uncle … and then with Nandu Uncle.'

Darshu felt his pain. She could only imagine how, as a kid, he must have spent the better part of his life without the care of his parents. Nothing could be worse than being forced to flee home at the age of eight.

Kanu continued speaking, breaking into sobs. 'I used to come to this temple when I was small. I was helpless. Nanu understood me. He wanted to keep me away from my uncles. He wanted to –'

Darshu tried to reassure him. 'It's not your fault. Don't let it overpower you …'

'Not being believed, that's the hardest thing. I know I couldn't have done anything. At least they could have believed me. I am sorry I get emotional sometimes. You are the only one who I could call –'

'Any time.' Darshu tried to smile. 'Everyone's pain is different,' she added. 'You must remain strong.' She touched his temple again. 'God! You're running a high fever! We must go to the hospital right away.'

'No, I'm fine,' he said, shaking his head from side to side. 'I'm fine. I'll call Bansi.'

Kanu pulled out his mobile and dialled Bansi's number, but when Bansi answered, Darshu snatched it away. 'Bansi, this is Darshu. Listen, Kanu has high temperature. He is shivering. Can you come right away?'

Bansi arrived in less than three minutes. 'Ah! You're in a bad shape, Kanu. I'll hire a car to take you to the hospital.'

'Should I come?' asked Darshu.

'I'll take care of him,' Bansi assured her. He promised to see an emergency doctor at Yashoda Hospital.

After they left, Darshu went up near the temple door. She put her hands together again and closed her eyes. 'Please make him strong,' she prayed.

Later that night, Darshu turned on her computer and typed in a search for 'Sathyamev'. It brought up about a million listings. As expected, the top results threw up some familiar information. She picked up a pen and started taking notes: *Sathyamev – established 1987 – co-founded by Rana Rajput and Samba Rajput – Employs 36,000 – IPO in 1992 – Market capitalization of Rs 23,200 crore –*

She then entered more search terms to know about Rana Rajput's business interests. One blog story written in 2003, among the many search results, interested her. A stockbroker had analyzed the phenomenal growth of Sathyamev. She read the article with interest:

> Call it Rana Rajput's magic or call it Sathyamev, the results don't lie. Sathyamev Computer Services has yielded a compounded annual growth return of 68 per cent every year for the past ten years.
>
> A single rupee invested in Sathyamev shares in 1992 returned 187 rupees in 2003. How amazing is that?

Let's see how it panned out for someone who had invested Rs 10,000 in 1992.

- Year 1992: You buy 1,000 Sathyamev shares @ Rs 10 per share in your name.
- Year 1999: The company declares 1:1 bonus, i.e., you have 2,000 shares.
- Year 2000: Stock split 5:1, i.e., you have 10,000 shares.
- Year 2003: Stock is trading at Rs 185 as of 23 December. The value of Rs 10,000 invested in 1992 is now worth Rs 18,50,000.

Now, add to it, the dividends earned in the ten-year period. Your total? Rs 27,920. That total today stands at staggering Rs 18,77,920.

A two-bedroom flat in a Delhi suburb is worth about Rs 12 lakh. Had you invested the small sum of Rs 10,000 in the Sathyamev stock a decade ago, you could have purchased the flat outright. No EMI. Now, what will you do with the left over chillar of Rs 6.7 lakh? How about going for a brand new sedan?

Does this sound incredible? Well, it's all happening! Right here, right now!

Then she tried a new search on the founders of Sathyamev. The results stated different information about Sathyamev's founders. In a few, she could spot the name 'Vasu Kumar' listed as a founder of Sathyamev. She sat staring at the screen. Tears began to roll down her cheeks as she recalled Kanu's story.

EIGHT

24–25 December 2006

The day after Christmas, Atul Ghoshal walked into Sathyamev's penthouse office to meet Rana without an appointment. A random visit from Ghoshal came once a year, always during the holiday season.

People close to Ghoshal called him Ghodal or a horse-racer, as he was always sprinting ahead of the pack. Ghoshal was the most sought-after trader and stock-market pundit in Mumbai. After running a renowned brokering house until he went solo in 1993, Ghoshal had averaged 49 per cent annual gains for his clients investing in the stock market. Rana had known him since the early nineties, when Sathyamev was listed on the Mumbai stock exchange.

'Good to see you, Ghoshal.' Rana rose to shake hands with the visitor. He at once noticed that his guest's tailored shirt and expensive suit coat couldn't hide the newfound bulge of a belly hanging over his belt. 'As I can see, you're taking good care of yourself.' Rana pointed to his belly.

'Festive season, sahib. Can't help it,' Ghoshal replied.

'So, how is HP? Are you still taking care of his business?'

'Ah, he is in a prison with all the amenities of a five-star hotel. But let me remind you, I'm not taking care of *his* business. I'm taking care of *my* business.'

'Is that your business or my business, Ghoshal?'

'It's our business. We have a word for it. Same-difference!'

'Yeah, same difference!'

While they both laughed, the fact remained that Harshad Parekh, or HP, the other golden boy of the stock market, had initiated the bull-run on behalf of Ghoshal. But during the liquidity crunch, HP was nailed and put up on the altar – his name became synonymous with the Madhavpura Cooperative Bank of India scam – while the real players continued with their business.

'You did well last year. But I must say, there are others who did reasonably better than you,' said Rana.

'Sahib, I know you are a hard taskmaster. You have information of our movements, but there's an adage that fits our generation better than any ...'

'Slow and ...'

'I was about to say relatively fast and steady ...'

Rana couldn't hide his smile. He knew he had a winner in Ghoshal. 'It's fantastic to see you again, Ghoshal. Always a pleasure!'

'Thank you, sahib! It's with your blessing that we are here.'

Rana drew out a file and placed it on the table. 'We are going to hit a bump this quarter. I know it's going to be less-publicized information, but you must know about it to take corrective actions. Have a glance at these figures.'

Ghoshal took out his reading glasses and studied the file carefully. 'Sahib, you can take over some company to hide this hole. Why make such a big fuss about real business when the market thinks everything is going well? The market will make the correction when it's required.'

'I was considering that option. But this time, I think, it's better to let it go.'

'You know more than I do.'

'Ghoshal, there's something else I wanted to talk to you about. It's nothing, really. A mere blip, I'm sure, and it has not reached the market. But I don't like bad news being published about us.'

'About the data theft news? In *DC*?'

'So, you've heard about it?'

'Yeah, I read it. I was thinking, is he the same guy who put up those figures back in 2001? Remember, when the results were accidentally uploaded on our website and other websites copied it ... markets slipped ... remember?'

Rana thought back to that day.

On 10 April 2001, it was reported that, due to a software glitch, the official website of Sathyamev had flashed its fourth-quarter results much before the financial results were approved by the board. Trade and news websites around the world saw the incomplete quarterly results and uploaded the same results on their websites. As expected, Sathyamev's shares fell sharply. Although the official homepage was fixed, the damage it did to the company's market valuation remained.

Rana stared at Ghoshal's face and shook his head. 'No,' he said. 'We should have known that something was missing from the story when we got hit by a technical glitch.'

Rana reached over to the intercom on his desk and pressed a button.

'Good afternoon, sir,' a lady's voice sounded out of the speaker.

'Can you ask Pranjal to report to my office? Ask him to get me the details of the 2001 website glitch.'

Rana paused to observe Ghoshal's reaction for a moment. 'Atul Ghoshal, you've made me reconsider a few things I thought were rolling smoothly. But we'll sort things out at our end. It was good of you to come!'

'Been a pleasure to see you, sahib,' replied Ghoshal.

Rana stood up and shook his hand. 'Keep in touch.'

In five minutes, Pranjal Hazarika was ready with his laptop to explain the origin of the website glitch in 2001. Samba Rajput had joined them as well. Pranjal stared at the screen studiously, avoiding Rana's eyes.

'Sir, websites cannot be hacked ... but sometimes they can be defaced ... or hacked. Our website is hosted on a secure server. The website management team, sir, is different ... so ... I will not know ...' mumbled Pranjal.

'You mean it can be hacked, right?' asked Rana.

'No, sir.'

'Are you sure?'

'Yes, sir ...'

'Okay, you can leave.'

'Thank you, sir.'

Pranjal left silently. As chief information officer, Pranjal had all the knowledge required to manage technical issues, but he lacked interpersonal skills.

Rana stared at Samba. There was a moment of uncomfortable silence.

'Samba, what kind of people do you recruit?' said Rana.

'You wanted a technically sound person to head the division. Somebody who does not poke around into others' affairs, right? This guy seemed to fit the bill.' Samba paused, as if he was unsure of his stance. 'I was thinking, is it possible that the technical glitch was an attempt to deface our website? Instead of leaving a hate message, Kanha opted to post our undeclared Q4 results?'

Rana's eyes hardened. 'He's turning into a threat. I've warned you before.'

'Like his father, he has first-rate programming knowledge.' Samba drew a long breath and continued, 'In fact, his entire batch at the NIIIT turned out to be hackers.'

'How do you know?'

'The SISI team compiled a report. There's another hacker by the name of Pankaj, who makes money from small-time hacks.'

'Is he a hacker like Kanha?'

'Both studied at the same centre.'

'I get your point. Let's set a thief to catch a thief …'

In less than four hours, Pankaj was at Rana's penthouse office. It was cloudy and a bit chilly that evening, even by Hyderabad standards. But inside the room, the temperature was precise. Pankaj was wearing a leather jacket and held a motorcycle helmet in his hand – looking quite out of place in the clinical corporate setting. He removed his jacket and slung it over his shoulder.

'You can keep your helmet on that table, there,' said Rana, looking at him warily.

'Nah, that's okay,' said Pankaj. 'By the way, thanks for sending a Merc. Nice ride! Someone said I was here for a website-related assignment?'

'That's right. We think our website was hacked in 2001 by your friend Kanha. I want to know how this was done, and if we can fix it,' said Rana.

'Kanha?'

'You may know him by the name of Kanu. His real name is Kanha,' Samba interrupted. He was seated on a sofa at the other end of the room, drinking coffee. Pankaj turned around. Samba sat up and continued, 'We have known him since he was a kid.'

'That's fine. We can discuss that later,' Rana said. He tilted the laptop screen towards Pankaj. 'This is my laptop. It has a password. Can you crack it? I'll give you thirty minutes.'

Pankaj smiled. 'Cracking passwords is for the films, Rana Saab. Your laptop has a login code with a minimum 512-bit encryption. More than a trillion combinations. This could be traced, but not cracked. If you give me access to your system with a fast Internet connection, I can tell you where your website is hosted, the platform it's built on, and the way its weakness can be exploited. Give me two hours, and I'll slow down your website so much it will take more than three minutes to load your home page. Even at 3.5 mbps. Give me twenty-four hours and your website will be gone …'

'You can *slow down* my website?'

'Ouch! I thought you knew?'

'Knew what?'

'Your entire bouquet of websites – what was it? Indiasomething.com? Yeah? The websites you owned were the target of a continued DDOS attack. The cyber squad didn't like your proclaiming that you bought a bunch of websites for what? Rs 500 crore? I think the DDOS began in 1999.'

'DDOS?'

'Denial-of-service-attack. Ah, distributed denial-of-service, to be exact! It's a syndicate that will overload your web server with too many requests. I can't believe none of your team members has informed you that your Allsify business was dying a slow death. The squad planted many unreliable contents on your website, killing your sites softly with love! Everyone in the IRC knew about it!'

'IRC?'

'Underground Internet Relay Chat networks. C'mon, don't tell me you don't know about IRC.'

Rana looked at Pankaj, his eyes wide. The bits and pieces of the Allsify business puzzle were connecting together.

At one point Sathyamev's subsidiary, Allsify, was the leading light of the online marketplace. It had acquired www.indiavishwa.com at an outlandish price of Rs 499 crore and the company was set on its mission to becoming *the* online value shopping mall of the future. Its stock price on the international technology stock exchange, Nasdaq, had galloped from an offer price of $18 a share to $174, bringing its valuation to a sky-high four billion dollars.

Unfortunately, the Allsify team couldn't figure out a way to monetize the hype. The gloss of ambitious acquisition and grand vision couldn't rub off the blotch: a loss of Rs 21.6 crore on a revenue of Rs 10.4 crore. The problems with the website's ranking and functionality persisted.

Allsify fell. And it fell big. In less than three years after the company went public, Rana was forced to write off huge investments in the loss-making subsidiary and sell off all his stake for the paltry sum of Rs 33 crore.

Rana could feel the heat on his face and a sweat breaking out. All his efforts had come to naught because of his own nephew. 'Samba, go smash that rotten kid!' shouted Rana. 'Allsify drowned because of him. I always knew there was something very wrong happening with Allsify.'

Samba got up slowly and walked over to Pankaj. 'Can you tell me who did it?' he asked.

'It's a coordinated attack. It's international. You can't even put blame on any single country, never mind a single person,' replied Pankaj.

'You're telling me there's no way to know if a person has done it?'

'Well, I guess it's possible, but that would require at least 50–100 dedicated computers. As I told you, your attack was more sophisticated and planned. They didn't take down your website. Instead, they just slowed it down.'

'Thanks, Pankaj. You're hired,' said Rana.

'But I don't want a job!'

'Why not? It's very well-paying.'

'I can't work in your nine-to-five environment. Programming is a craft. It's rigorous. You can buy the artwork but you can't buy the artist. If you buy the artist, you kill the craft.'

'That's fine. Your place. Your work hours. Your craft. My money.'

'That sounds like a deal.' Pankaj thumped his fist on the table.

NINE

27–31 December 2006

At 10.15 a.m. on 27 December, a man wearing a hooded black jacket walked into the SJR Canteen near Sathyamev's Ojas Tower in Secunderabad. He took a corner seat and ordered a coffee as he fiddled with his mobile phone. When he left the place, a box containing several floppy discs occupied the seat he had been sitting in. A few minutes later, a man wearing dark, thick-rimmed glasses and a buttoned-down shirt collected it and silently slipped out of the canteen.

Kapil Sharma, a twenty-three-year-old programmer and one of the brightest interface designers at Sathyamev, sat alone at the Karkhana branch, nursing his thoughts over a warm cup of espresso. A voice intruded on his thoughts.

'Kapil Sir, there's a parcel for you,' the office boy said, handing him a package.

'For me?' asked Kapil.

'Yes, sir. This box was delivered in the afternoon at the reception.'

Kapil studied the shipping label. 'Artwork? Any idea … who delivered it?'

'No, sir. They didn't inform.'

'Okay, I will check …'

Around the same time, a junior Sathaymev technician received an unexpected parcel at his desk through SpeedFast Courier Services. The sealed envelope attached to the parcel had an introductory note: 'Norman Antivirus Update.'

He tore open the envelope and pulled out two CD-ROMs. He inserted one into the CD drive. Immediately, his system went into auto-run mode. Instead of opening the correct folder, the system displayed a blue screen and, after 30 seconds, rebooted with an additional desktop shortcut icon – Norman Antivirus Update.

Kapil sat at his desk with a zip drive in his hand. The printed instructions prompted him to insert the zip drive into his system and check the content. As he did so, a folder containing a 'PSD' document – Sathyamev1_artwork.psd – appeared on the screen. He double-clicked the file, but instead of opening the file, the system shut down.

Kapil quickly restarted his machine after ejecting the disc. But the system functioned abnormally slow. With a landline phone receiver to his ear, he dialled the helpdesk number.

'Hi, this is Kapil. Can you send someone to the Design Studio to check my system? It's responding very slowly. Thanks!'

He put down the receiver, thinking the zip drive may have contained suspicious files.

But Kapil didn't know that the malware on his system had triggered a highly sophisticated, self-replicating version of itself that was now taking control of other connected systems.

Within minutes, the malware controlled hundreds of computers at the Karkhana office.

The Sathyamev Karkhana office branch had just three tech support personnel along with their supervisor, Badal Singh, and they were being overrun with requests.

The computer crisis became the talk of the office. Everyone, from the top boss to the data entry staff, wanted tech support to fix their problem first.

The list of lodged complaints varied: *My navigational folder doesn't open; my Word document is taking forever to open; my Excel crashed without warning; my browsers jammed up in between navigation sessions.*

The Karkhana office was in disarray, while Badal Singh shuffled among the employees.

At 12.30 p.m., Kanu called the Karkhana office landline number and punched the extension for the tech support section.

'Tech support,' came the female voice, accompanied by a clattering sound from the keyboard.

'Hi, this is Govind, from the Norman Cyber Security office. I spoke to Mr Pranjal Hazarika. He asked me to get in touch with the IT supervisor. Can you tell me who handles IT in your branch?'

'Badal Singh,' replied the representative.

'Yes, Badal. Sorry, I forgot his name,' apologized Kanu. 'May I know your name, please?'

'Shirisha,' she replied.

'Can you put Badal on the line?'

'No, sir. He's on the third floor. There's a critical issue, which is why ... He'll be back in about thirty minutes.'

'Okay, then can you ask him to get in touch with me when he returns? Or, even better, can you give me his cell phone number?'

'Sure, sir! Please note down ...'

When Kanu called Badal Singh's mobile number five minutes later, he introduced himself and mentioned Pranjal Hazarika and Shirisha by name. 'A short while ago I spoke to Shirisha. I understand you guys are facing some kind of crisis. Could you describe exactly what's happening?'

Badal felt helpless as he confessed the problems at hand. 'Yeah, there's been some kind of malware attack. Our designer put a zip drive that contained malware into his computer. It's starting to spiral out of control.'

'No problem. At Norman Cyber Security, this is exactly what we specialize in. Can you tell me if you are in front of the computer right now?'

'Yeah, I am.'

'Do you have access to FTP?'

'Yes, I do.'

'Please disconnect and log out from the network connection. FTP is not the place where you want this malware to move. First, we must isolate it from spreading to other drives. But before we do that, can you tell me if you are connected to the Internet?'

'Yes, I am. Should I disconnect from FTP?'

'Please do that first. The next thing you should do is download a file from our Norman Cyber Security website. Google search for "Norman DDS 9612-patch". It's executable. Run it and change the password settings on your system.'

'What is the file again?' asked Badal.

'DDS 9612-patch.'

'Yeah, it's showing. Should I click on this link?'

'As long as it's on the Norman webpage. Do you see it?'

'Yes, it's there,' Badal replied.

Kanu had worked meticulously to make sure the webpage extension had the look and feel of the original Norman webpage. Even the domain, with the long URL of the scam website, matched the original. There was no way Badal could have noticed the difference.

'Are you there?' Kanu asked.

'Yeah, give me a minute ...'

'Take your time. I'll stay on the line. Reboot your system after running the file. You will get your system back,' said Kanu.

Back at the Karkhana office, Badal leaned forward as the monitor turned black and rebooted. The display screen lit up with the Windows start-up chime audible in the background. Badal entered his recently changed password, and the familiar Mickey Mouse wallpaper appeared on the screen along with the other desktop icons. The newly-opened menu notified that the computer had been cleaned of 22 malware files.

Badal opened a few folders and the response time seemed normal. He clicked on a browser icon and the website home page loaded up in no time.

Relieved, Badal spoke into the handset. 'Everything is up again now. It all seems to be working. Thank you so much ... your name again, please?'

But the line was dead.

That very moment, Kanu turned his attention to a small window that looked like a 'command-prompt' dialogue box. He had secretly established an interface with the malware-infected system at Sathyamev. His machine was paired with administrator privileges. Kanu could impersonate a keyboard and enter text on his own computer without Badal's knowledge. On Badal's screen, everything looked normal.

Kanu opened the FTP folder 'SYS-KAR' that housed the Karkhana's employees' folders. A massive vault of information was his for the taking.

The two flat-panel monitors on his desk indicated that files from the replicated screen of Sathyamev's office – the one containing the Mickey Mouse wallpaper – were being moved into an anonymous folder.

The next morning, when Badal turned on his monitor, he did not, at first, understand the reason behind the mysterious message: *Files from SYS-KAR had been moved to Anonymous. Press OK.* He pondered over the notification for a while before pressing *OK*. He then opened the SYS-KAR folder, but it was empty. The Karkhana employees' files were all gone. 'God! There's no data ... it's all gone ...' he panicked. 'This is gonna kill us ...'

A secret meeting was convened at Sathyamev's nineteenth-floor conference room in the early hours of Thursday morning. The secrecy was motivated in part by the reluctance to concede that Sathyamev's systems could be easily penetrated and in part by the fact that they were terrified of breaking the news to Rana Rajput directly.

Samba Rajput presided over the meeting attended by Venkatesh, Pranjal and Badal. Their goal was to determine how to bring back the infected systems to a normal functioning level.

'How long do you think, Pranjal, it will take to partially restore the network? I believe this is the day our investment in backup servers will come in handy. Is that right, Pranjal?' asked Samba.

Pranjal, feeling his professional survival was at stake, stammered, 'I'm sorry, sir. I do not blame Badal. But it's only human –'

Samba didn't let him finish. 'Oh! Shut up, Pranjal. How many times will you say sorry? I don't want to hear that. I want to know your plan of action –'

Venkatesh took over. 'I believe the contingency plan is in place and being acted upon as we speak. By now, a large majority of our systems will have received a login notification to back-up files. We've personally called and requested all employees to refrain from leaking the news – even to the drivers and security personnel. I am sure this can be contained within two hours.'

'Could this have been led by a disgruntled employee, maybe one facing a pink slip?' asked Samba.

'Blaming an employee would be too easy. People would say we're just trying to hide our shortcomings. All evidence suggests otherwise. The revelations and chronology of events as narrated by Badal should leave us with a good idea as to who was behind this attack. The caller who had identified himself as the Norman Security representative must have done this,' said Venkatesh.

'Let's do this ... let's track him. But, for now, let's finish the task at hand.'

The meeting was adjourned as the team scattered to act on the contingency plan.

The team in the conference room was only going to break the news to their CEO after partially restoring the system. But Rana, who was back in Hyderabad, had known about the cyber-attack all along.

He was furious when he learned about the meeting that had taken place without his knowledge. He went straight to Samba's office to confront him.

Samba defended the meeting, adding that it was only to assess the initial damage. 'Ultimately, we were going to inform you. We wanted to ensure that the news is contained, which is also why we met so early,' he said.

But Rana was not convinced. Immediately he summoned Samba's assistant to the office. 'Sheena, get me Pankaj's phone number – the hacker guy. Samba knows about him. And send a memo to Pranjal. He's no longer required. Also, keep tracking news sites. If there's any negative news on Sathyamev, you call me immediately. You have my number.'

'Yes, sir,' Sheena replied.

Kalimbhai, one of the drivers of the Mercedes entourage, was sipping tea alongside Rafiq, the security personnel posted at the Ojas Tower building. Rafiq was an old employee of Sathyamev and was concerned about the recent shake-up.

'I've seen Samba Sir and the others running around between different offices. What's the matter? Is something wrong? I've never seen them so stressed out. Are they under attack or what?' asked Rafiq.

'Someone is using a brute force against them,' replied Kalimbhai.

'Brute force?'

'I heard it from Driver Kaka. The Rajput brothers were discussing the matter while they were returning home in their car. Driver Kaka told me as much. This may seem unbelievable but it's happening.'

Rafiq looked on in anticipation as Kalimbhai sat up to give an account of what he understood of Kanu's cyber-attack.

'They say he's a computer whiz. He comes in the dead of night when bats rule the sky. He's visible for a moment, then disappears into thin air. He's young, but no one knows who he is. He can fly from one tower of the building to another – just like that – hands held out like wings. He chooses his own targets. Flames do him no harm. Smoke accentuates his presence. When he is gone – you can see the office up in flames. He's brutal. He's invincible. He is the almighty of our digital world.'

Rafiq shook his head in wonder. What Kalimbhai said must be true.

'He's left behind crumbs for us to follow. Phone number. User logs. IP addresses. Zip drive with malicious malware. And a dummy Norman webpage with the domain registered to one Chuck Norris. I don't think Chuck Norris will be of any help, but all the other leads can surely help us trace who he was,' said Pankaj.

Pankaj was sitting in Rana's office and spoke with the authority of a leader. 'I must say you lack the basic – I mean level-one – security infrastructure. But I have a question. How valuable is this stolen information? I mean, can someone monetize the information?'

'No, I don't think so,' replied Rana.

'Do you know what RAT is?'

'Pity we couldn't defend ourselves,' said Rana, lost in his own thoughts.

'I know it must be upsetting. But I assure you we can do better. Here, these IP logs can give away the location of the cyber-attack.' Pankaj pointed to the screen of his laptop. 'I told you I have a copy of this programme so this makes it easier to trace the origin of the attack. But there's one thing I must admit. He is more powerful than all you guys put together! In one hour, he totally had you under his control.'

'I run an empire,' declared Rana. 'And in my empire there's only one rule. *My rule*. Anyone disrupting my rule must go.'

'Now you're talking like a boss!' Pankaj smiled.

Rana reached for the intercom and activated the speaker mode. A ringing sound could be heard from the speaker before a voice answered. Rana wasted no time in giving his brother instructions.

'Samba, you call Bhardwaj and tell him to come to my office –'

'– Bhardwaj? You mean Superintendent Bhardwaj?'

'Yes, tell him I want him in my office immediately. Connect me to the chief minister's office. And listen, we are setting up a command room, here in the office. One more thing, I want to leave a video message for Kanu.'

TEN

27–31 December 2006

Kanu knew he needed a better way to store and back-up Sathyamev's digital files. He was also sure Rana and his team would eventually figure out the origins of the attack. The first piece of evidence against him was the command and control IP addresses hidden in the malware. Also, instinctively, he knew Rana would set his men after him, even before getting the forensic report of the malware.

Kanu couldn't stay at his place and visiting the cyber café meant putting Bansi at risk.

Only one man could help him.

Kelkar was at his desk reviewing his students' paperwork when Kanu walked in.

'Good to see you, Kanu,' Kelkar said. 'Have a seat. Look at these papers! No one is interested in learning these days ...'

'Sir, I need your help.'

'Yeah? Tell me.'

Kanu placed the hard disc on Kelkar's desk.

'What is this?'

'Sir, I need help linking these files to this server.' Kanu pulled out a piece of paper with a handwritten web address and a password code. 'These are compressed and password-protected files. Around 3 GB of data.'

'You look a little worked up. Is anything the matter? Please have a seat.'

'No sir, I've some unfinished work. Got to go now.'

Kanu stepped inside the waiting auto rickshaw and instructed the driver to take him to the Secunderabad railway station. As the rickshaw sped down the busy S.D. Road, Kanu felt a vibration in his pocket. He pulled out his cell phone and saw an incoming video message from an unknown number. Without thinking, he hit the OK button.

'Good work there, Kanu …' Rana gave a discreet smile as he appeared on the mobile screen, '… if you try to damage my business …' Kanu pushed the pause button below the screen.

'Can you please stop the vehicle?' he shouted. As the rickshaw stopped, he stepped out, chest pounding, hands tightening on the handset.

Rana's presence on the screen was hazy and disorienting, partly because of the moving vehicle, but partly because of the buzzing in Kanu's head. Now, out in the open, Rana sounded even more menacing: 'If you try to damage my business, I will destroy you. You know the one that sits in a wheelchair. If you try to kill my business, I will kill you.'

Kanu's gaze remained fixed to the mobile screen, his hands closing over Rana's face as the screen cracked into pieces. The image of Rana vanished behind broken glass.

At 6 p.m. on Friday, 29 December, the Hyderabad police released mugshots of Kanu. The suspect was charged with 'aggravated kidnapping' of a twenty-one-year-old girl called Rita Shah. It was believed Superintendent Bhardwaj's office had made a special arrangement to trace and arrest the suspect.

Almost immediately, police spread out across Secunderabad. Simultaneously, they raided MNR Cyber Café and shut it down. A dedicated battalion patrolled around Kanu's last known residence.

Kanu studied the traffic movement. There was no indication of Rana's men on the street. Still, he knew the streets were too dangerous for him, day or night.

Earlier that evening, he had made a call to Bansi's number, which went unanswered. Now Kanu feared the worst. *Would they try to harm Bansi?*

Kanu dialled Bansi's number from a pay phone. On the fourth ring, Bansi answered.

'Yeah?'

'Bansi, it's me.'

'Where the hell are you? Listen, I am outside the police station. They shut us off. Now these people are searching for you. I think they broke into your house too. You are wanted for kidnapping a girl.'

'Kidnapping?'

'Yes, kidnapping. I am at the police station trying to get details from the officer. Listen, there's a warrant against you.'

'How can they issue a warrant against me?'

'I can't say more right now. Where are you?'

'I'm on my way.'

'No ...'

'... don't even think of coming anywhere close to this area.' Bansi's voice was being recorded in a hastily set up three-screen computer command centre at the nineteenth-floor conference room. Two technicians wearing red uniforms worked on computers that displayed hundreds of numbers. One number in particular was prominent on the screen, creating continuous waves in sync with the voice audible over the speaker.

'Shit, man! How could anyone charge me with kidnapping a girl? They're framing me!'

'You took on a bunch of big people – these people are criminals. I got to go. You take care, buddy.'

'Listen, you don't worry about a thing. I will call when I am in a position to –'

The line disconnected, and the oscillating waves stopped.

Rana stood alongside Pankaj, taking note of the voice messages.

'Can you trace Kanu's location?' asked Rana.

'No, he is calling from a fixed line. We can track the other guy's location,' replied Pankaj.

'Okay. Let's keep a watch on the other guy. Kanu will definitely contact him again. This control room is yours,' Rana said.

Kanu emerged from the pay phone booth and approached the waiting rickshaw, but the wailing sound of an ambulance made him turn around sharply. A shudder crept down his spine as he saw the vehicle, its lights flashing, storming into a park lane that led to the CTC Complex. In no time, the ambulance wailed its way back out of the premises. Kelkar?

When Kanu reached the place, onlookers were discussing the standoff at the NIIIT office.

'What happened? Please, somebody, tell me what happened?' Kanu asked.

'They took Kelkar to the hospital. It all happened so fast,' said one onlooker.

'I could hear the noises, but I couldn't do anything,' replied the fifth-floor security guard. 'I came in from the classroom, but before I got here, they had already beaten him up bad.'

The shopkeeper from the adjacent shop spoke up. 'They had guns and ordered us to stay inside. They wore helmets. It was all over in a minute. They collected the money from the desk and fled.'

Kanu examined the ransacked office and the upturned desk drawer. The disc was gone.

Kanu could see a couple of men looking at him intently from the side of the open corridor. He was being shadowed. There were more men moving outside.

Kanu slipped out of the building as silently as he could. Out in the open, SISI men were on the lookout, trying to close in on him on the busy street. But, before they could cross over, Kanu disappeared into the darkness.

From a distance, Kanu could see Bansi waiting next to several parked taxis near the Secunderabad Rail Nilayam. As he approached the taxi stand, he noticed his friend shouting, rising on his toes, his hands waving.

Kanu could barely hear Bansi's voice, but the gesture was unmistakable. He slowed his pace and held his breath as he began to turn around.

Suddenly, he heard the sounds of a harsh slap followed by a scream from behind. Kanu spun around to see a young man wearing a long coat kneeling beside two motionless bodies. In a flash, the man in the long coat had overpowered two uniformed men and he was clearly ready for more.

Kanu tried to run in the opposite direction, but the voice of the man in the long coat made Kanu stop in his tracks.

'Kanu, you've made plenty of enemies. That's not a good sign.'

Under the floodlights the man's face looked familiar.

'Bala?' mumbled Kanu.

'I was tracking the SISI phone chatter. One of them was instructed to finish you,' said Bala as he walked towards Kanu.

'Bala!' Kanu gasped.

'Even now you don't recognize me, do you?'

'I'm so happy to see you. Where have you been?' Kanu lunged forward to hug his elder brother.

Bala had always been the stronger brother, even when fighting the school bullies. In Kanu's world, Bala was a hero, and his presence meant things were looking up.

Bala was three years older than Kanu, and they were more than just brothers. They were childhood friends. They grew up in the same house in Kompally and studied in the same school. They played gully cricket together and fought battles like real WWF wrestlers. They saw the world through the same eyes until their father, Vasu, decided to send Bala to the Dhoon Boarding School. Bala was barely ten. In the same year Vasu established Sathyamev Computers.

As the years went by, the brothers hardly met. Bala had only come home once since the tragic incident involving their father. He believed everything Kanu said about the incident. But the circumstances were different. No one in the family cared to listen to the boys.

'Railway Nilayam, where wagons are repaired, you couldn't pick a better place to meet?' said Bala.

'I wanted to leave a message before it was too late,' said Kanu.

'Leave a message?'

Before Kanu could reply, Bansi had reached them.

'Bhai, nice kick! That was super cool, just like in computer games,' he said.

'Bansi, this is my brother, Bala,' said Kanu.

'There's no time for introductions, Kanu.' Bala looked concerned as he glanced around the empty street. 'What's your next move? We don't have time.'

Just then, a crash echoed through the quiet street. A car had smashed through the barrier, and they could hear gunshots coming from its direction.

Bansi hunched behind Bala to shield himself, as Bala took cover behind a car in the parking lot.

Kanu realized this was not the time to fight back. He ran to the top of the staircase that led to the platform, just as a train thundered past him, too fast to board. But there was another train waiting on the tracks, ready to depart.

Kanu knew what he had to do. He called out to his brother and ran towards the train, trying to push open the door of an AC coach. Before Bala and Bansi could reach him, Kanu was already inside the coach. Stretching his hand out, Kanu pulled them in.

No one gave chase.

'The city is not safe for you. You have to get out of here,' said Bala, looking at Kanu.

'Will you come with me?'

'It's your fight, Kanu. I'm here only to support you.'

'I'll never understand why you take sides. This is not just my fight. It's our fight.'

'Mom and dad are with me, you know that. He is not well.' Bala shook his head as he continued. 'There are two ways to approach this situation. Pull your enemy's tail and continue this game of cat and mouse. Or be with the family and take care of them. I chose the latter.' Bala was always the stronger of the two. He was the adopted one. He had more responsibilities.

'I know I may be irresponsible ...'

'You are brave. It's your destiny to do the right thing.'

'But Sathyamev has grown way too big. I've tried everything. They just keep growing bigger and stronger.'

'Remember, it's only Sathyamev that can bring down Sathyamev. The company will kill itself,' replied Bala.

Kanu looked at his brother, trying hard to make sense of his advice. Bala smiled and nodded his head. 'You're doing the right thing. Here, this is a card of a man who can help you in Mumbai. He's a stock market analyst. Take care.'

Kanu did not look at the card. He hugged Bala and then Bansi as the train slowed near Begumpet station.

'Bansi, this is for Darshu.' Kanu pulled out a handwritten note from his pocket and gave it to Bansi. 'I couldn't meet her, please say sorry on my behalf.'

'You take care, buddy, and call me whenever you need any help.' Bansi smiled before walking out of the coach.

Moments later, Bansi and Bala stood silently on the platform as the carriage disappeared round the corner of the station.

ELEVEN

One year later
6–31 December 2007

Kanu leaned forward, his elbows up on the hard, white marble surface of the reception desk at the Hotel Royal-Hilton in Mumbai. He was wearing a fashionably-tailored gray suit, buttoned-down white shirt and a navy-blue tie, slightly loosened at the neck. A leather messenger bag hanging from his shoulder made him appear like a businessman, an outsider to the city.

'The room number is three-nought-six,' Kanu said, looking at the receptionist. 'Can you help me with the coffee-shop Wi-Fi password?'

The receptionist smiled.

'Sure, sir!' she replied. Then she scribbled a number on a pad and held out a piece of paper to him. 'Here, this will be your passcode. Rates are mentioned on the back. Can I get your signature on the copy, please?' she said.

Kanu pulled out a pen and signed the copy – Sarvasya, a new name Kanu had picked during his stay at the hotel. The receptionist studied the signature and smiled. 'Thank you.'

Minutes later, Kanu was inside the coffee shop and saw the place for what it was: a group of young men gathered around the billing system, a middle-aged white man staring at his laptop, a young couple sipping their lattes while staring at the screens of their mobile phones.

Silently, Kanu pulled out his laptop and a small black device – no larger than a regular mobile phone – from his leather bag. As he powered on his machine, punching keys to log in and connect to the network, tiny red and blue lights blinked on the device. Soon Kanu could read 'Coffeeshop Poolside' and 'PC&A Notebook' on the network window of his laptop screen. The black device, although small in size, was intercepting the signals he needed.

For the next few minutes, Kanu worked on his laptop with surprising speed and grace, the soft instrumental music in the background blocking out the tapping of keys. In less than ten minutes, he had learnt everything there was to know about the white-skinned foreigner sitting with the laptop.

The man, Julian Covey, was an influential hedge-fund manager of a US-based multi-strategy private asset management firm called Panther Capital Advisor. Though the firm was registered with the stock market regulatory body its managers had been embroiled in controversies for their alleged role in insider trading. From his intercepts, Kanu learnt that the mandate for

Julian was simple: dump banking stocks and liquidate their position, irrespective of market conditions.

Kanu opened his mailbox and sent an encrypted e-mail to an unknown group. His message was simple and did not include any justification. 'Get rid of all ICICFC and all other banking shares. PC&A to liquidate their position today.'

Later that morning, Kanu strolled away from Hotel Royal-Hilton, his black leather messenger bag still hanging from his shoulder. All that the two guards watching the surveillance camera feeds noticed was the familiar sight of a tech yuppie walking out of the coffee shop with one hand in his pocket and a black leather messenger bag slung over his shoulder.

Outside, an ambulance wailed relentlessly at being stuck in traffic, while on the sidewalk a group of college girls stood underneath a large umbrella eating masala corn and giggling.

Kanu stood there, as if waiting for somebody. Soon a shiny black BMW pulled up next to him. He opened the rear door, tossed his laptop bag inside and slid into the car.

TWELVE

6–31 December 2007

The voices and chatter were impossible to ignore, and they seemed to grow louder with every passing second. Under ordinary circumstances, these distractions wouldn't have made Darshu lose focus. As a copy-editor of the *Afternoon Times*, her morning stint at the desk consisted of revising copies for the afternoon pull-out. She sat in her cubicle dressed in a collared white shirt under a black sweater and a pair of blue skinny jeans.

Eventually, the growing chatter made her turn around. Almost all her colleagues had gathered around the desk of Kiran Shah.

Kiran was a senior business correspondent of the *Afternoon Times* and had pulled up the trading terminal from a wire that gave instant trading positions from the Mumbai stock exchange.

'I just don't believe this. It's a vertical drop,' Kiran exclaimed, pointing to the screen that displayed a moving graph. His personal laptop, right next to it, although slow in reporting positions, flashed the breaking news from the CNB website: *Stock Exchange down 400 points*. 'It's actually 485 points down and it's still sliding,' Kiran shouted.

'What's happening?' Darshu asked, as she reached Kiran's desk to get a better understanding of what was going on.

Nobody spoke except for Kiran's shrill cry. 'I've never seen it this bad. The stock market is down 500 points in just three minutes! The market is baked!'

'500 points down?' Darshu asked.

'Yeah, it's touching the depths of Niagara Falls!' a cheerful voice from behind said. It was Suhail, a young reporter.

Darshu stared, mouth agape, as the readings on the screen went down from 510 points to 530, then 577.

The graph on the terminals didn't make sense. The downward movement every millisecond resembled the movement of the stock market. 'Now it's 620 points down. It's madness,' exclaimed Kiran shaking his head.

The other reporters who had gathered around Kiran's terminal were also trying to figure out the mystery.

'RILL is down 4 per cent. Sathyamev is down 10 per cent. ICICFC Bank is down 15 per cent. Would you believe this? 15 per cent down in three minutes flat!' came the cheerful voice of Suhail again.

Suhail hovered over Darshu's shoulder. He enjoyed watching the market go boom and then crash. Today was his lucky day.

'Sathyamev is down? How much did you say?' asked Darshu.

'87 points. It must be more now. But look at all the banking stocks. Collectively they just shaved off 20 per cent in a matter of minutes!' said Suhail.

'It's mayhem out there!' Kiran exclaimed. 'Thankfully ... have they suspended the trading? Yup! This is going to be one of those days I use to explain to my kids why not to invest in the stock market.'

Just then a middle-aged lady in a purple sari tapped on Darshu's shoulder. 'There's a phone call for you on my landline number. Some guy. Keanu?'

'Hello ... Darshu here.'

'Darshu, this is Kanu,' the voice answered. 'So good to hear your voice.' Kanu paused. He was calling from the comfort of a luxury car, cruising through the Queen's Necklace in Mumbai. 'Hello? You there?' He paused again.

'Yeah, I am listening. Is that really you, Kanu?' she said.

'Hey, how are you?' he said.

'Hey, I am good. Thank you. How have you been? What took you so long to call?'

'I was in Mumbai. Wanted to meet you. How about Goodies outside CST Station, that's where your office is, right?'

'Okay.'

'See you at two, during the lunch break.'

'Okay.'

Before she could say any more, the line went dead and Darshu was left holding the receiver. She kept staring at the receiver, distracted. *Figure out the stock market collapse or meet Kanu? Why did the market collapse so suddenly?*

* * *

Seen from a distance, the Goodies Restaurant didn't look like much, especially considering its small entrance on the ground floor that led to the main dining area above. But, of the many food joints on the street, Goodies served authentic Gujarati dishes, making it the most sought-after place for office-goers.

By the time Darshu reached, it was already 2.35. She walked inside the restaurant and realized the man sitting alone, wearing a grey suit, tie and shiny black boots, was in fact Kanu. *Whatever happened to his jeans?*

Kanu caught her eye and stood up, grinning. She flashed a smile but only shook his hand, a little unsure how to greet him.

'Thank god! You're here,' she said. 'Look at you, how have you been?' The smile never left her face as she pulled out the chair opposite him.

'Good. I can't believe you're here. Where have you been all this while?'

'In Mumbai. What about you?'

'Different places.' He smiled. 'Have a seat. What will you have?'

'Thanks.'

The waiter approached the table just as Darshu was about to take her seat. 'Would you like to have a bottle of mineral water?' the man asked.

'Yes, please,' replied Kanu. After the waiter had left, Kanu looked at her, eyebrows raised. 'I've been waiting and waiting. I thought you wouldn't come. You are late by forty minutes.' He looked at his wristwatch and then his cell phone. 'Now, forty-two minutes!'

'You didn't give me a phone number to call you back. What was I supposed to do?' she said.

The waiter appeared with a bottle of water. 'Would you like to order something?'

'So, what will you have, Darshu?' Kanu asked her as he glanced back at the waiter. 'We'll let you know in a minute.' Then, very earnestly, Kanu leaned forward to inform her. 'I thought you wouldn't come, so I *ate!*' he whispered.

'You what?'

'Look at this place.' Kanu threw his hands up in air. 'They wouldn't let me sit here without food on my table.'

'That's so mean. You called me for lunch and you couldn't wait?'

'Look at this man.' Kanu pointed at the waiter who was busy collecting menus from the nearby table, not far away. 'Do you think he would have allowed me to sit here without stuffing my face?'

She glanced at the waiter, who looked more like a bouncer from a movie. 'Okay, I'll forgive you this time.' Then, turning to the waiter, she called out, 'Excuse me.'

'Yes, Ma'am.'

'We'd like to have, um, two paav-bhaji and two mosambi juices.' Then she glanced back at Kanu. 'The second one is of course for you.'

'Thanks, but no thanks!' he said after the waiter left. 'So what are you up to these days?'

'I am with the *Afternoon Times*. Been a long time. You know how it was in Hyderabad.'

'I know.'

'Those were tough days. Every day in the office I had to pretend that things were normal. After my story on Sathyamev, our editor got himself a plush car! I know what must have happened. Soon after I started looking for a job and this is where I landed.' She poured water from the bottle into one glass and then the other. 'So you are on a business trip? I mean, here in Mumbai?' She slid one glass in his direction.

'Thank you,' he smiled. 'I live here.'

'You live here? Really? How long have you been here, Kanu? At least you could have called me.'

'Almost one year. But I don't stay anywhere very long.'

'Where do you live?'

'As I said, in Mumbai.'

'Yeah, where in Mumbai?'

'Do you really want to know?' He paused and stared at her with his eyebrows raised, like she'd asked the wrong question. 'Why do you want to know?'

'Okay, if you don't want to tell, forget it!' she said, laughing.

Kanu felt bad about jumping all over her, but he had his reasons. 'Remember, the last time when we met it was the sixth of December? Your article was published a day before?' he said.

'Really? You remember that –'

'And today is the sixth. That's the reason I called.'

'You mean to say, you waited for this day to call me?'

'Why else would I tell you this?'

'C'mon, you could have called me any time.'

'Yeah, you're right. But things were –'

'You don't have to explain,' she said, not quite looking convinced with her own statement.

The waiter arrived with two plates of paav-bhaji and two glasses of juice, placed everything in front of them, and went away. Darshu turned to Kanu. 'The food looks good. Let's see if it tastes just as good.'

'It's delicious. This is the second time I'm eating it!' He smiled.

'So what is it that you do?' she asked.

'I am a stock market analyst, um, rather a hedge-fund manager. I think stock market analyst is a better term?'

'Really? What are you doing out here? The market just crashed – you are in the wrong place!'

'Yeah, you're right. But I've a team. I can afford a day out.'

'So you are the boss,' she said, nodding her head mischievously.

'Yeah, see that shiny car outside? On the other side of the street?'

'The red one?'

'No, the black one.'

'Yeah.'

'Well, that's not mine.'

She smiled. 'Okay?'

'But I can rent a luxury car for a day or two. I earn a decent living. No complaints.'

'So you're are stock market broker, but you don't work, 'coz you have a team and you can hire a chauffeur-driven car. Am I missing something here?'

'You're a damn good detective. You're hired!' he said as they both started to laugh.

Kanu's phone rang, interrupting their conversation. He didn't answer it right away as he considered the name flashing on the screen. 'Sorry, I have to take this,' he said before speaking into the device. 'Yeah, Sandhu?' Kanu paused to take in the information. '455. It's still high. I think it will go down further. We did our bit, now we just need to keep tracking Ghoshal's move. You know what I mean?'

Kanu put the phone on the table and picked up the juice that came with their meals.

'Did you notice the unusual movement in the stock market today? It's a vertical collapse! It's more than 600 points down in a single trading session.'

'Now it's down by over 1,000 points. But it will recover close to 600 points before the close.'

'How do you know that?'

'Know what?'

'That the market will recover?'

'Wild guess. And there's something called margin calls? These promoters and companies will do everything to bring back their valuation.'

'Hmm, so you know a great deal about the market,' she said. 'I think Sathyamev stocks are also falling sharply. Banking stocks were hit the worst.'

'I know.'

'It all came back to me when they were talking about Sathyamev today. It's a coincidence that you chose this day to call. How have you been?'

'Life is good. Sathyamev is doing what it does best. Pushing numbers.'

'Kanu, you're still upset?'

'Not sure ...' He looked away.

Darshu wanted to ask, but figured it was best to leave it alone.

It was 3.20 when the waiter returned with the cheque. Kanu raised his hand, gesturing that the bill was for him.

'It was nice of you to come and meet me after all these years,' said Kanu, putting the money in the folder, cash sticking out. 'You know how it was ...'

'Yeah, I know ... I am so glad to see you too!' she said.

Since she arrived at the restaurant an hour ago, she had remained oblivious to the world around her. Now she was out on the street again.

'Mumbai. This is my place. I feel like I belong here.' She glanced over her shoulder. 'But sometimes when I open my e-mail account, I have this nagging fear someone might be accessing it.'

'What are you looking at me for?' He smiled.

'Have you been looking through my e-mail?'

'No. Why would I? I have my own work.'

'I know. Just that creepy feeling.'

'Do I look like a creep?'

'It's not –'

'Your office is not far away. Can I walk you to your office? I mean, if I don't sound like a creep already.'

'You don't have to ask.' She smiled.

They walked along South Mumbai Street, and then turned left towards her office. Their walk didn't last for more than five minutes. Kanu looked up at the towering *Afternoon Times* office, then at his watch, before fixing his gaze on her.

'It didn't feel awkward, really, to walk you to your office,' he said, eyes still on her. 'Now, don't look at me like that. I'm being honest here.'

'Whatever.'

'No, I mean it. I don't know … I just feel there's so much to say. You know? Lots of catching up to …' He looked at her uncertainly.

She was smiling.

THIRTEEN

6–31 December 2007

The next afternoon, Darshu was at her desk when Mrs Desai walked up to her with a scornful look on her face.

'Who is this Keanu Reeves guy? He's on the phone again for you, Darshu,' Mrs Desai said.

'Thanks!' said Darshu as she hurried to take the call.

'Yeah, Darshu here,' she said, picking up the receiver.

'Hi, it's me. Lunch at two? Same place?' Kanu said.

'Can you call on my mobile? My boss is getting angry.' She smiled at Mrs Desai who had returned to her seat.

'But I don't have your number.'

'Okay, I'll give you my number when I come. And don't finish your lunch before I arrive!'

The conversation lasted just a minute. When Darshu put down the receiver, she winked at Mrs Desai. 'Yeah, you're right. He's the same guy from *A Walk in the Clouds*!'

'I hate you!' Mrs Desai smiled.

Kanu was waiting for her outside Goodies amid the busy commuters of CST. He seemed to be enjoying the Mumbai winter, wearing a grey sweater over a grey checked shirt and navy blue pants.

'Hi,' said Darshu extending her hand to him. 'Thank god you're not inside stuffing your face.' She gestured to the entrance. 'Shall we?'

'Hey, hold on. We're not going to Goodies? Are we?'

'You invited me to Goodies, didn't you?'

'Yeah, I said Goodies. But that man inside? You know, if it were possible, he would force me to finish my food in two minutes, take away all my money and then throw me out.'

'Now you're being grumpy. What's wrong with you? C'mon!' She tried to shove him in the direction of the restaurant.

'How about Taj?'

'*Taj*? That's on the other side of the city.'

'But it's only a nice ten-minute ride away!' He looked at the car in front of them and motioned. 'That car you see there, that shiny black one?'

'Yeah, it's not yours.'

'Right, that's the one I've hired today.'

'We have a young waiter for a change,' Kanu whispered, as a young man in a bow tie and a white jacket approached them.

'Good evening, Ma'am, Sir,' he said, handing over the menu. 'Let me know when you're ready to order.'

'Thank you, Kamlesh. We'll let you know!' said Kanu.

The waiter disappeared into the kitchen. The lighting at the Taj was subtle and warm, the temperature just right, and business news played quietly on a TV screen in a corner.

Kanu leaned in. 'Did you notice how polite he was?'

'Did you notice the price column in the menu?'

'Point taken.'

She stared at him as if he were a stranger. 'You know what? I have a new name for you. Keanu Reeves.'

'Hmm, I must get those black shades of mine. Where did I lose them?' Kanu searched his pockets.

'Don't! Here, this is my card.' She slid her business card with the title of copy-editor under her name. 'And you can call me on this number.'

Kanu studied her name carefully. 'I never told you this before. My house in Secunderabad was just a hundred metres away from your office. I often saw you and thought, "Who is this girl?" Then you showed up at our shop.'

Darshu shook her head, trying not to smile. 'Some memories.' She looked around the restaurant. 'Do you come here often?' she asked. 'I noticed you called our waiter by name.'

'You know, we have business meetings here sometimes.' He looked at her. 'Speaking of business, did I tell you that in the stock market crash yesterday, I made close to twenty lakhs in a day's trade?'

'Twenty lakh rupees, you mean?'

'Yeah, twenty lakh rupees.'

'Are you trying to impress me or what?'

'Honest. I'm not making this up. Twenty lakhs – that's just my share.'

'I don't believe it!'

'I swear. I can show you my account.'

'No, you don't have to!' she said, shaking her head in disbelief. 'What kind of business are you in?' She was quick with her next question. 'Can I get a job there?'

'I can recommend your name!'

'Please do that. I shouldn't be saying this, but in print, the salaries are so low, it's not fun any more. Tell me, what's the name of the firm you work for?'

'BizzareBazzar.com. But that's just the advisory website. I handle the portfolios for different hedge funds.'

'Come again?'

'Never mind. You probably won't understand.'

'No, seriously, I want to know. Where's this office? Bizarre, what did you say?'

'BizzareBazzar.com. It's in Vile Parle.'

'You're still doing hacking work, aren't you?'

'Practically, no. I am an analyst. So, getting information beforehand can be helpful. But no, I don't hack!'

'You "get" information, but you don't hack?'

'I snoop around – that's not hacking.' He looked around and leaned in again. 'That's one level down. But don't tell this to anyone.'

'Don't tell me, you go after information to manipulate the markets.'

'You're bang on, detective!'

'That's not funny,' she said.

'Ma'am, that's the way it is the world over. There's a price to every piece of information.' Kanu spoke slowly, deliberately. 'If you must know, information is being monetized by corporations. They cheat innocent investors. What do I do? I bring out the information – hidden information – much before the promoters would –'

'You mean you get insider information and trade it. Is that what you do?'

'No. I monetize information. Let's say, some mysterious promoter of some listed company is having a secretive deal about his business. That's not cool. It's *not* his money he's playing around with.'

'So you go after information.'

'Don't say it so loudly out here. As I said, there's a price to every piece of information.'

'Gosh! This is unbelievable.'

Kanu leaned back in his chair with a glass of water in one hand, his gaze steady on Darshu as the waiter cleared the table and left.

'You're not judging me? Are you?' he asked.

'No, I mean, it's bizarre. And your firm's name is BizzareBazzar,' she said uncertainly, 'so that justifies it!' She tried to force a smile.

'I shouldn't have told you. But basically what I do is trade information. Legal information.'

'No, that's perfectly okay.' She looked at him intently. 'And where do you stay? Oops, sorry! You didn't want to share.'

'These days I am in Santa Cruz West. Been there for almost three months now. But I don't stay in one place for very long.'

'What do you mean?'

'Okay, okay, I confess – I stay in a hotel.'

'Really? Isn't that expensive?'

'No, actually, it's cheaper. And convenient. I am single, so one room is enough. The two-bedroom flats here are no bigger than a lavatory. I mean, if you compare it to Secunderabad. And the rent is 35k. Then there's maintenance, electricity, maid – so many additional expenses. At the hotel, you give them an upfront payment for a month and the room charges come down by fifty per cent. No electricity. No maintenance.'

'Amazing! Somebody should do a profile of you!'

'You tried once!' he smiled.

FOURTEEN

6–31 December 2007

A chopper hovered before landing on the rooftop of Sathyamev headquarters in Madhapur at 11 p.m. Rana Rajput stepped out of it on to the grey concrete. He wore a black suit and dark glasses, despite the odd hour of his visit.

Rana strode to the control room on the nineteenth floor where Pankaj stood staring at the images on a giant screen in front of him. He turned back to greet his boss as he heard the sound of the door opening.

'Pankaj, what's the latest? Get me every detail,' Rana barked. 'Only bullet points.'

'We've found him,' Pankaj said. 'He's in Mumbai.'

'Good, good! Show me, what have we got?' His lips curled into an evil smile.

Pankaj leaned forward to observe the image on the laptop. The giant screen above replicated the same image – green, spectral-shaped signals in a waveform. It started oscillating and the speakers in the background accurately reproduced the amplified sound: *Kanu* ...

'That's the voice of a lady.' Pankaj looked at Rana and then back again at the small monitor below the larger screen. 'And that's a positive match. We will play it again, this time a little longer version.'

I met Kanu yesterday ... I don't believe ...

Pankaj clicked the pause icon as the recorded female voice overlapped with the second female voice. Rana turned his attention to the giant screen, moving in a little closer.

'And who are these girls?' Rana asked.

'The first one is the reporter girl. Remember, the girl who broke the hacking story?'

Rana nodded. 'Who is the other girl?'

'Some girl, Ritika. Not important. Let's hear it again.' Pankaj leaned forward again to play the recorded voice: *Kanu ...*

He picked up a mobile device from the desk below. 'My programme can intercept conversations in real-time, twenty-four seven. I always knew he would contact this reporter girl sooner or later, and I knew she was in Mumbai. Her phone number was on my intercept list. The programme intercepted the voice-match and the alert showed up –'

'When was that?'

'It's been about ten days,' replied Pankaj. 'Don't worry, I've set our men to dig out his details carefully. The result may surprise you.'

'In a good way? In a bad way?'

'In a bad way, I think. He started a website – BizzareBazzar – that publishes investment tips. Not a groundbreaking idea, you might think, but there's a catch.' Pankaj's voice was slow, steady. 'He has programmed an algorithm to trick the market into believing that his offer is the best. As the market keeps moving to his best offer, the algorithm keeps changing the best offer price. Probably he wouldn't buy any stocks, since he wasn't offering the best price; he's only spoofing. His big offer is just an illusion. More like dangling a carrot in front of a donkey, only that the carrot here is a 3D image. The donkey, mind you, is real.'

'Stock market traders?'

'Exactly.'

'He's coiled himself around your business as well, squeezing it ever so slightly.' Pankaj looked at Rana to assess his reaction. There was none.

'Go on, I am listening,' Rana said.

'Don't worry, Sathyamev's online security is impenetrable.'

'Yes, you've done a good job. So what's the plan? You didn't call me just to break this bad news?'

'We've installed CCTVs everywhere. Nobody knows when these cameras were installed or why. There are thousands of cameras that the government hasn't installed, so we took the initiative on their behalf. Here, this is what we have captured so far.'

Pankaj opened up a dialogue box and soon one image after another filled up the giant screen. The photos showed Darshu and Kanu in a coffee shop, outside her office, outside her home and strolling in a busy street. One photo in particular showed them under the shade of a giant tree, sipping fresh coconut water. The time stamp at the bottom of screen read: 7.35 a.m.

'Looks like he's steady with this girl these days,' Rana said.

'It took me eight days to piece it together. Things are normal, as you can see. We'll take it slow, then swoop in with all our force. We'll take him out before anyone can notice.'

'Remember, no matter what you do, there should be no trace-back.'

'It would all be automated.'

'I always knew we invested wisely in you. Good work, Pankaj. Give me updates after you have cleared up the mess.'

'Right-o!'

FIFTEEN

6–31 December 2007

At 7.15 a.m. on 24 December, Darshu and Kanu walked side by side through Joggers' Park in the direction of the 120-foot-wide, tree-lined road that connected Gokul Towers Road with the Western Express Highway in Kandivali. Soon they reached a pushcart vendor, who had stacked coconuts by the pavement against the walls of the park.

The vendor was a short, gentle-faced man and appeared to be in his mid-fifties. After slicing off the top of a fresh coconut with a large knife, the man punctured the fruit and offered it to Darshu, along with a straw. He offered the second one to Kanu.

'I won't need a straw,' said Kanu to the man. 'Thank you.'

Darshu shook her head, looking at Kanu.

Kanu smiled. 'What?'

'Nothing,' she said.

'Why are you looking at me like that?'

'Why do you always want to be different?'

'Now, what is it *this* time?'

'I'll never understand why you prefer to drink coconut water straight, without a straw. It looks so silly.'

'Did I ever ask you why you sip it through a straw?'

'You better not!' she said, sipping her coconut water and eyeing him mischievously.

'Let me tell you, with a straw you bypass your taste buds. If you don't want to believe me, that's fine. But if you start following my style, you'll never go back to sipping through a straw, ever!'

'Okay, challenge accepted. But don't laugh if I spill.'

Darshu gripped the fruit with both hands and gulped a mouthful, her face to the sky.

'Did you feel anything?' he asked.

She lowered the fruit. 'I can't breathe,' she gasped.

'You don't have to finish it in one go. Should I get you a glass or something? Even a glass is a better option than a straw.'

'No, that's okay.' She began chugging the fresh coconut water again. 'Wholesome ...' she breathed.

'Slow down, champ!' he said.

'Hey, what's that?' she said, pausing mid-sip. 'That flying thing?'

Kanu followed her gaze. About 150 metres above them he saw a hexacopter with a moving camera-like device mounted on its belly. The mechanical bird hovered over them for a brief moment and then glided away, disappearing from sight. Kanu's voice was shaky as he pretended not to have seen the flying object.

'Don't look up. Something's wrong,' Kanu said.

'What?'

'Someone's shadowing us. Let's move. Now –'

But before Kanu could finish, he saw an ambulance speeding towards them from Gokul Towers Road.

The vehicle had no driver.

'Run!' he yelled over the screech of tires and the roar of the engine.

The vehicle smashed through the vendor's cart into the concrete wall, a few feet away from them. Kanu looked back to see the cart vendor pinned against the wall, his arms splayed out in front of the vehicle.

'Don't look back. Keep going,' Kanu said, holding Darshu's hand as they fled.

'No!' Pankaj screamed as he sat back and ran his hands through his hair.

In a tiny control room in Sathyamev's Guest House in Malad East, not far away from the Joggers' Park, Pankaj sat in front of three monitors displaying different views from the crash site. None of them made for happy viewing. The first camera feed from the CCTV mounted outside Joggers' Park showed Darshu and Kanu disappearing from the frame. The second camera feed, a view from inside the ambulance, was jammed up, showing only a black surface. The third view displayed random aerial images.

He had planned it all in such detail. But now a terrible feeling of dread overwhelmed him as he hunched over, looking down at the controls of his console. He then tried to manoeuvre the long-view camera from outside the park in an attempt to follow the fleeing couple.

'Do we have a backup here?' asked Pankaj, turning to Kapu, his assistant. Kapu stared into a blank-looking computer screen, his hands busy with the keyboard and the remote that was laid on the desk.

Kapu was an old accomplice of Pankaj's who operated from Mumbai. He was on the wanted list issued by Interpol in connection with an online Canadian bank fraud and had teamed up with Pankaj as a programmer on various other projects.

'Why is this camera blank?' asked Kapu, instead of replying.

But Pankaj was not listening. 'Where's the drone eye?'

'The drone's circling. There's no problem with that. The bloody van is stuck. It's not even moving in reverse,' shouted Kapu.

'You idiot, use your brain,' yelled Pankaj.

For nearly two years, Pankaj had worked on the radio-controlled unmanned aerial vehicle design to complete the prototype he had retrieved from Kanu's computer. Pankaj's new programme for the prototype was designed to sync the hexacopter's movement with the self-driving vehicle. The remote application was able to do just about everything – from changing direction to avoiding obstacles to returning to the launch centre after each mission – without any human intervention. Now, Pankaj could see his own failure magnified on the screen – a blank camera feed that showed nothing.

Next to him, Kapu struggled with the radio controller. 'I can't move it,' Kapu shouted again.

'Race it forward and then try reversing it. It's stuck somewhere.'

After a brief moment, Kapu was able to manoeuvre the vehicle again. 'Yeah, it's moving now.'

'Quick, the crowd's getting anxious,' Pankaj said, looking at the screen. 'We need to dump the vehicle immediately.'

Back at Joggers' Park, people had gathered around the crashed ambulance. On finding no driver in the vehicle, a man shouted: 'It's a terrorist attack. Run, there's a bomb in it! Run!'

At 3.30 that afternoon, Darshu and Kanu were in the elevator of Regency Airport Hotel along with a young attendant in a white jacket carrying a small suitcase. The hotel was one of the busy stopovers in Vile Parle East that catered to travellers needing a place to rest in between flights.

Kanu had booked a double-bedroom suite on the fourth floor under the name of Paarthsarthi and had identified himself using a driving licence registered in Maharashtra.

On reaching the room, the attendant unlocked the door using the digital key card.

'Sir, hope you'll like it here,' he smiled.

'I'm sure,' said Kanu. 'Do you have an Internet connection in here?'

'Yes, sir. You can call at the reception to get the password,' the man said as he switched on the lights and the air-conditioner.

Kanu poked his head into the bathroom and briefly inspected the room. Satisfied, he came back and gave a generous tip to the young man.

'Thank you, sir!' the attendant said, smiling broadly. 'You can call me whenever you want. I can get you anything, anything you may want.'

'Thank you,' replied Kanu. 'I'll let you know.'

Kanu waited to hear the steps of the man walking away before bolting the door. Then he paced back to where Darshu stood. He had seen her standing helplessly at the hotel reception, trying to get a grip over herself. Maybe she was stunned beyond words.

He reached for her, enveloping her in his arms.

'You okay?' he asked.

'Yeah,' she said, her voice muffled against his shirt.

'I should have told you this before,' he said, moving back a little to see her better. 'All this while, I've been trying to run down Sathyamev. Something must have given them the idea –'

'Who *were* they?' she asked, looking into his eyes as he let go of her.

'I don't know.'

She searched his eyes. 'Did that man die? That man in the park?'

'I don't know. He was injured –'

Kanu moved towards the television screen mounted on the wall. He picked up the remote from the tray and turned on the set.

'Are they coming after you?' she asked.

Kanu did not reply as he flipped through the news channels. The ticker that ran across the bottom of the screen screamed the breaking news: *One person left dead and two injured by an unknown ambulance in Kandivali.* He flipped over to another news channel reporting live from the site.

A female reporter appeared on the screen and started speaking: 'A coconut vendor was killed and two others were injured when an out-of-control ambulance crashed into a pedestrian lane in Kandivali early this morning. The rampaging ambulance crashed into the vendor's cart, right here, where I am standing. This place is near Gokul Towers complex. But mysteriously, no one saw the driver of the ambulance. We spoke to an eyewitness who said the vehicle was without any driver.

'We will run a clip of that interview shortly but I will read out what he said. He said that when he reached the site, moments after the crash, he saw no driver in the vehicle. But another eyewitness said the driver was popping his head up now and then to see the road. Perhaps the killer driver wanted to hide his identity. We also spoke to a police officer who said they are conducting an enquiry about the vehicle.'

Kanu glanced at Darshu. He could tell she was fighting to hold back her tears. He turned off the television and reached for her, his left arm draping around her shoulder. 'I know all this sounds so terrible, but trust me, this will be over soon.'

'Is it because of *me* you always get into trouble?' she asked, as tears started rolling down her cheeks. 'Last time, when I wrote that piece in *DC*, you were forced out of Hyderabad. Now, in Mumbai again ...'

'Don't worry. It will be okay. Remember what I said. We have to be safe for a few days. That's all. Are we okay with this arrangement?'

She nodded, though she realized with some discomfort that she didn't have much choice. Strangely, she also found herself grappling with the fear of losing him again.

'I get anxious when I think of the people who are targeting you. They –'

'Don't be,' Kanu smiled. 'I was born on Janmashtami. That's why my name is Kanha. In short, Kanu. My mom always said I am her hero – and a hero always wins.'

She turned to look at him again. Finally, she smiled.

Seven hours after leaving Sathyamev's guest house, a battered vehicle rolled into the underground parking area of the building. There was no indication that the vehicle had been without a driver or that it had remained parked behind several abandoned vehicles not far away.

'Ambulance is back in its base,' said Kapu.

The vehicle could be seen in a surveillance video of the hotel that Pankaj monitored. He took out a handkerchief and wiped the sweat from his face.

'That's one part of the story. Now let's make sure that the drone is also back before it's too late,' Pankaj said.

Pankaj had employed drones for surveillance purposes before. But this was his first experiment with two different vehicles, controlled and operated from a remote location to strike off an enemy.

'I think the battery died. There's no GPS signal,' said Kapu.

Pankaj was not pleased. He punched a few commands on the keyboard with no success. He knew there was little he could do to regain control of the lost device.

Kanu was focused on this laptop, studying the satellite map of Joggers' Park. He sat in a padded fabric chair, a few feet away from the bed where Darshu was curled up asleep. There were practical problems he had to resolve before he could consider rest.

Kanu remembered being followed by some kind of metal device that spun in circles, but it had disappeared suddenly near a lamp post in the Evershine Dream Park. Did the metal bird crash into one of those light poles? Google Maps calculated the distance between Joggers' Park and Evershine Dream Park, where they hid during the attack.

Kanu smiled. He had connected the missing dots of the puzzle.

An hour later, Kanu drove past Viceroy Park that surrounded the Joggers' Park campus and headed towards

Evershine Dream Park. He stopped at a garbage dump, far away from the busy street, and tried to determine where the drone might have crashed.

After a while, he stepped out of the car and strolled some distance away to another dark green dumpster. It was here that he saw the crumpled metal piece on the ground, just beneath the lamp post. He collected the pieces and calmly walked back to his parked vehicle.

On the way back, he stopped at a hardware store to get himself the tools required to realign the unit. He bought batteries, solar panels, blades, an adjustable-ratchet, screwdrivers and other essential equipment.

Kanu carried two big shopping bags in his hands when he reached the hotel room. When he stepped in, he saw Darshu had a water bottle in her hand and was looking through the newspaper laid out on the table.

'Look what I've for you! A new phone with a new number,' Kanu said as he pulled out a box and handed it to her.

'Where have you been? I was worried,' she said. 'What's that, the other bag in your hand?'

'It's a drone. The same thing that chased us in the park.'

'What are you doing with it?'

'It's broken. So I'll fix it.'

'Fix it? Why would you do that?'

'Coz I am taking back the control of this technology,' he replied.

The next morning at the control centre of Sathyamev's guest house, Kapu could see a shaky image on console trying to light up the black screen.

'The drone is coming back to life,' he informed Pankaj. 'The batteries must have realigned. I have seen drones bounce back after collisions before.'

'Who is that kid holding it?' Pankaj asked, looking at the image carefully.

'Must be some street kid. He must think it's a toy.'

'Can it fly? Can you bring it in?'

'Yes, it's in flying condition.'

'Great, bring it in!'

Somewhere in Viceroy Park, a kid in a soiled, unbuttoned shirt was playing with his new toy helicopter. Suddenly, it slipped from his hand with a jerk and, instead of falling on the ground, started to manoeuvre its way up in the sky. The kid looked on surprised as the toy disappeared from the horizon.

Moments later, the same kid ran towards Kanu, who was observing the drone's flight on his laptop.

'I let the toy fly in the sky, like you told me,' beamed the kid.

'Here's 500,' smiled Kanu, as slipped the money into the kid's hand.

A pixelated image of browns and grays escaping the tall buildings of the city could be seen on Kanu's laptop screen. Minutes passed, and the flying object inched closer to a five-storeyed building in Malad. It circled for a while before landing on the terrace of the same building.

The images showed a man pick up the device and carry it to a room, where Pankaj could be seen sitting at a computer. Kanu watched as his enemy picked up the device and tried to inspect the camera.

'Happy birthday, Pankaj,' said Kanu as he pressed the Enter key.

A white flash of flame blossomed on the screen.

At the control centre at Sathyamev's guest house, a deafening explosion tore through the fourth-floor room. A huge fireball blew out of the windows, shattering the panes, as shards of glass and bone fell to the street below.

SIXTEEN

5–12 July 2008

In a dimly-lit conference room, a middle-aged presenter stood staring silently at a screen that displayed a slide outlining Sathyamev's financial performance in the North American market. The graph showed a 20.6 per cent growth in the last quarter.

There were six executive board members seated around a conference table. A bespectacled man in a dark-blue business suit leaned forward, nodding, and then he gently tapped the table in appreciation. The other members followed suit, happy with the company's performance.

But Rana, as the leader of the group, wasn't impressed with the figures. He sighed and shifted his gaze from the cheery board members to look at the presenter.

'Yes, yes. That's all very good. What's your name again?'

'Subhramanium Swamy, sir. I'm the head of the North American market,' came the reply.

'That's all very good, Subhram Mani. But do you know how the stock market works?' This was, as usual, a rhetorical question. The boss wasn't expecting an answer.

Rana then glanced over at the group of three sitting at one side of the conference table and repeated the question.

'Does anyone here know or understand how the stock market really works?'

The board members glanced at each other nervously, troubled by Rana's displeasure.

As was expected, none replied.

'Raise your hand if you've heard the latest gossip of a hostile takeover of Sathyamev by IBMM,' said Rana.

This time, everyone present in the room sheepishly raised their hands.

'If everyone here knows about it,' Rana continued, 'maybe it's not a rumour. It's news, then. Isn't it? If you must know, our stock price rose more than 12 per cent in the first week of November based on that rumour. Yes, you heard it right – 12 per cent. But more surprising is the fact that it came down by about 36 per cent – *36 per cent* – the very next day after we issued a statement denying this rumour. What does that mean?'

There was dead silence in the room.

'What does that mean?' Rana persisted, but nobody was willing to reply.

'Last year, Sathyamev's stock price has shed more than a quarter of its value, 38 per cent to be precise, despite coming good with the numbers. How do you justify losing 38 per cent of our market value? I am asking you, mister,' Rana looked at the presenter, 'whoever you are, how do you justify that?'

The presenter lowered his head and remained silent. By now the fear of Rana was beginning to spread through the group. The board members had seen Rana lose his cool before and had known things to quickly turn nasty.

Luckily for them, Samba, sitting next to Rana, stood up and whispered something into Rana's ear.

Rana nodded, then swung his feet up on the conference table, leaning back in his chair. The bespectacled board member in the dark-blue business suit looked on passively, trying hard not to stare at Rana's shiny shoes.

Rana looked around at the board members, and then eyed the same bespectacled board member in the dark-blue suit.

'Gentlemen, the stock market doesn't give a shit about what you do. Or what your friend here does. All they care about are the numbers. And that's what we'll be doing. Giving them the numbers. Now, coming to the previous question, did IBMM try to buy us out? If you must know, it could have been a rumour. But one thing is sure: we survived only because of our big-time investment in our own infrastructure company, VEMAYHTAS. That was like a poison-pill for IBMM to swallow.'

VEMAYHTAS was a privately-held construction and infrastructure development company, its name was Sathyamev spelled backwards in capital letters. It was Rana's pet project and was widely accepted as Sathyamev's twin company.

'You will learn all about our strategy for the expansion of VEMAYHTAS in the dossier on your desk. We've also prepared a press release about our decision to invest a part of our surplus cash in acquiring lands in Hyderabad under our subsidiary VEMAYHTAS.'

The board members looked at each other in astonishment. But as was the tradition at Sathyamev's board meetings, all decisions were based on what Rana wanted as opposed to the company's mission statement of what business demanded.

Rana stood up finally. 'You guys can carry on with the presentations. The software business, as you can see, is doing just fine. The press release is drafted and will be issued to the media on your behalf.'

Turning to Samba, who was sitting next to him, Rana said, 'Samba, come, let's go. The board has plenty of presentations to take care of.'

The board members looked on – a few of them rising from their seats to show their respect – as Rana and Samba left the room.

'What's happening, Samba? Why am I feeling so low?' said Rana as he flipped the lever under his office chair to raise himself. Rana was in his penthouse office occupying his usual seat while Samba sat opposite him.

Samba had seen his brother make some weird moves, change his decision in a matter of minutes, act like an eccentric dictator. But on this day, he was sounding defeated. Perhaps it had to do with the news trickling in from Mumbai.

'Pankaj was an idiot. He could have asked for our support but he didn't. He paid the price for being overconfident,' said Samba.

Rana was deep in his own thoughts, too engrossed to hear his brother. 'Last night I woke up to the sound of beeping monitors laid out in a hospital. It was as if the prophetic voice of that fortune teller was coming true. I was in a hospital bed, fighting for life,' said Rana.

'The voice? That was ages ago. You still remember the words of that fake fortune teller?'

'His words have remained with me forever. Strange, I can still recall them so vividly.'

'You don't have to worry. We are combing each and every hotel in Mumbai. I phoned the chief minister's secretary, Jagjivan Reddy, yesterday. He said he's assigning Kanu's case to a special wing of the CID. There will be no slip up this time.'

'We shouldn't have let him escape when we first found out about him. Look at the damage he has done to our business. All these years, he's been at our neck, hurting us. First it was Allsify. Now it's Sathyamev. Look at this report sent by Ghoshal. Last week, I asked Ghoshal to prepare an in-depth report on the BizzareBazzar.com business model. This is what he has mailed me.'

Rana slid his laptop towards Samba. 'Read it aloud, and I will help you understand what it means.'

Samba carefully studied the screen and then began reading:

Dear Sir,
There exists an elite group of stock market analysts who can raise the market or make it drop, simply on the basis of their move or recommendations. As you must have observed, BizzareBazzar.com is one such financial entity. Its mailing list includes no less than 2000-odd big-time traders. The website's recommendations hold value and acceptance among the subscribers, mostly because of the novelty and accuracy of its recommendations. They seem to know beforehand about almost every move that the stock market will make hours, sometimes days, in advance. In fact, a number of subscribed traders said that based on the mailing group recommendations, their stock picks have returned 158.6 per cent (as of 20 December 2007) since they first started at the end of January 2007. The stock market mid-cap index, by comparison, gained just 15 per cent. Now the question is, what's the secret to these market-disruptive recommendations? On their website they say that they make recommendations after much deliberation, in-depth research and testing it across multiple algorithm models –

Rana interrupted Samba. 'Hacking. He hacks into the system and steals information that no one else is aware of. He can get direct access to the CEO's e-mail. He knows what's going on, what's going to happen next. Okay, read on.'

Samba continued:

> *In reality, it's all insiders' information. In our tumultuous times, they seem to know what's about to happen. Or perhaps, they understand the stock market so well that they can manipulate the market before it takes corrective action. They know how to create greed and how to instil fear, just by passing on the information –*

'Yes, it's all about *information*. Now, imagine who in this world could have authorized or paid for this ridiculous study, *Implications for future growth if IBMM were to buy out Sathyamev* by JPM consultants? Imagine JPM being part of the rumour machine. This kid is playing some real pied-piper tunes.'

'So this suggests that Kanu is hacking to dig gold from the stock market? Perhaps, devalue Sathyamev's stock?'

'What more evidence do you need? Look at the money I lost because of the pressure on margin call? It's more than 6 per cent of my Sathyamev's shareholdings.'

What bothered Rana was the disparity between the price at which he pledged a major portion of his shares as collateral with banks (at a weighted average price of Rs 420) and the current stock price level of Sathyamev, which was trading at Rs 322. It was agreed that if the closing price of Sathyamev's share price were to fall below Rs 420, such an event would trigger a margin call and Rana would have to provide cash, or cash equivalent top-ups, to compensate. Rana had tried every trick in the book to ensure that the share price did not drop below Rs 420. But still Sathyamev's prices kept sliding, trading at Rs 310–340. As the share fell below Rs 420, banks started placing increasing demands on Rana to cover margin calls. The only avenue left for him was to pledge additional Sathyamev shares. The margin call trigger had left Rana with less than 6 per cent of Sathyamev's equity.

Samba rose from his chair. 'This explains a lot of things. Could we –'

'Sit down. There's nothing we must do in a hurry. The damage is already done. And our investment in VEMAYHTAS is not half as bad. The only money that's hurting is the cash we raised to pay to the chief minster's son to start his media empire.'

'Yeah, I agree.'

'But on a positive note, the bribe money and official support bagged us all government infrastructure projects for VEMAYHTAS. Today our landholding is worth thousands of crores. It's better than Sathyamev at this point. I think even after bribing politicians, we are making a killing in real estate.'

'What about the Sathyamev shares that are already pledged?'

'Do you know what "intangible" means?'

'You mean "intangible", the word?'

'Yes, the word.'

'Intangible means not real or something that you can't feel.'

'Exactly. Sathyamev is in the business of intangibles. It's all in zeros and ones. They call it software development; I call it zeros and ones. My Allsify was valued at four billion dollars at one point. Then it became *zero*. VEMAYHTAS is in the business of realty. It's real. They call it real estate; I call it our future opportunity.'

Samba looked at his brother. 'What about Kanu? We can't have him do more damage.'

'He cannot. We have hedged our bets by acquiring more land. The stock market may go down; realty never will.' This time Rana rose from his chair and walked to the edge of the glass window overlooking the Sathyamev campus. 'There's this three-day NASSO IT conference in Pune. All we have to do is ensure my keynote is well-publicized all over the country, including Mumbai. Kanu will come flying like a honeybee.'

'You bet!' Samba smiled.

'But this is not just any desk – it's the desk on which I, Kanu, Kanha, um, I'm working on. This desk will go down in history as the desk that was used for 38 hours by Kanha. There will be auctions for this desk in years to come,' said Kanu. He had been on his laptop for hours, which had not gone down very well with Darshu.

'Yeah, it's called a garage sale. Not auction,' Darshu said.

'That's insulting.'

'Are you coming or do I have to go all alone, again?'

'Okay, I'll listen to you just this once. But I'm still your boss. Remember the agreement.'

'Yeah, that you are my boss and I work for your PR firm.'

'And?'

'It's not just any PR firm; it's Biz-Bazzar PR firm that promotes www.BizzareBazzar.com. Are we done?'

'You know the drill. What about the elevator pitch I asked you to prepare?'

'Hi, I'm Darshana Soni, vice president, business development, for Biz-Bazzar PR,' Darshu began methodically. 'We tie together business stories from government offices, manufacturing units and industries, so you get to know what's making news. And we have our own website that's bizarre enough to make you stand up and take note of what's making news. It's *biz dot bazzar dot com*. Here's my card. Maybe we can set up a time to meet and talk about your business needs and get your company to make some positive news? And my job already sucks. But the money is good. Otherwise, I'd have never taken up this offer.'

'Yeah, my job sucks too, but you are perfect!' he said.

Thirty minutes later Darshu and Kanu were at High Street Mall – a premium shopping area with a wide, palm-lined street with swanky stores, galleries, restaurants and gaming zones – in Lower Parel.

'Damn, that's something,' Darshu exclaimed, looking at an advertisement that had Rana's face plastered on a huge billboard looming above. 'It seems Rana is invited as a chief guest at the NASSO IT conference in Pune,' she said.

Rana's thin, inviting smile, coupled with the text below, gave away the hidden message. *This is your last chance to meet the legendary Rana Rajput in person*, the artwork proclaimed.

Kanu stood back and looked at the poster with intent. 'Yup, time to make a visit to Pune,' he said.

SEVENTEEN

5 January–12 July 2008

In the early hours of 15 February 2008, the reception area of Gulmohar Taj Hotel, a 120-room luxury hotel in Pune, was silent except for the swish-swish of a uniformed cleaner mopping the multi-coloured marble floors. The entrance doors opened and a young man dressed in a sky-blue uniform wheeled two bulky suitcases to the front desk.

'Good morning, sir,' the smiling receptionist said. 'Welcome to Gulmohar Taj.'

'Good morning. I think, my admin has made a reservation for our stay. Here, this is my business card,' Kanu said, sliding his visiting card on the marble surface of the front desk. 'Could you please check?'

Kanu was dressed in a tailored black suit with a white shirt and a black necktie. He hadn't removed his dark glasses, even inside the dimly-lit lobby. The receptionist clicked the mouse and peered into the monitor below.

'Mr Radha Krishna from Biz-Bazzar PR?' she asked without looking up.

'That's correct.' Kanu smiled. 'And she is my companion.'

Kanu looked over his shoulder and saw Darshu walking towards them. Darshu flashed her widest smile as she came towards the desk.

'Hi, I am Darshana Soni.'

'Good morning, ma'am, welcome to Gulmohar Taj,' the receptionist said. She tapped on the mouse again, her eyes scanning the monitor for more information. 'The reservation is for five days. Is that correct?'

'That's correct,' said Kanu. 'We had asked them to book two separate rooms on the same floor.'

'Yes, sir. It's B-402 and B-406 on the fourth floor,' the lady replied.

'I believe we've made advance payments for this?' Kanu asked.

'Yes, sir,' replied the lady as she extended a white-coloured plastic card with a black strip on it. 'Here's your key, sir,' she added.

Kanu nodded and collected the key. The room number printed on it read: B-402.

The receptionist then looked at Darshu and extended another card with B-406 printed on it. 'Ma'am, this would be for you,' she said.

'So kind of you,' said Darshu. 'My other luggage is in the vehicle. Can you get someone to deliver it to my room? I've got to prepare a presentation for an event. It's going to be a long day,' she said sheepishly.

'Sure, ma'am,' smiled the receptionist.

'Great, see you around,' Darshu said as she strode towards the elevator, Kanu following closely behind.

An hour later, Darshu and Kanu were at the Holiday Villa Hotel, about fifteen kilometres away from Gulmohar Taj, on the outskirts of Pune. It seemed as if every media person in the vicinity was passing through the hotel lobby on that day just to make sure they were invited to the wedding reception of an influential couple from the film industry.

Kanu stood in line to check in, his ID and address proof in his hand, while Darshu pulled her luggage along behind.

'Sir, can I have your ID proof?' the receptionist asked when Kanu's turn arrived.

'Yeah, sure! One ID proof is enough for both of us?' Kanu said pointing to Darshu, now seated in the lounge area. 'We're together.'

'No, sir,' the receptionist replied. 'We would require a separate photo-ID proof.'

'Not a problem,' Kanu smiled. 'I've got IDs for both of us.'

It took less than a minute to finish the check-in procedure. Kanu grabbed the luggage Darshu was carrying and headed straight to his room. When he returned to the lobby five minutes later, he had a laptop bag with the familiar Norman Cyber Security logo printed on it. His suit jacket and tie were gone and he had rolled up the sleeves of his white shirt.

Darshu was already waiting for him when he reached the hotel exit.

'I did some research about our work. Guess what? They will charge me for being *an* accessory to your crime,' Darshu said in a low, disgruntled voice.

'Really?' Kanu smiled.

'You really think I'm that dumb?'

'You really think I'm a criminal?'

Kanu and Darshu were whispering together as they walked through a sliding door into the hotel that was about to host the NASSO IT conference. Life-size banners announced the keynote address by Rana. It was obvious that the luxurious hotel, Western Koregaon Park, had ensured the best of security arrangements to welcome its delegates.

'Okay, is this security for you? Or am I being too imaginative?' she asked.

'Hmm, that's a good question. We are three days too early. So, to be honest, they aren't expecting me yet. Besides, there are so many other things the organizers must take care of. Don't worry, these guys have a lot on their plate,' he said. He then motioned for her to secure an empty seat in the lobby towards the back of the room.

It was not unusual for Kanu to frequent luxurious hotels without any reason or appointment or to take part in a business meeting uninvited. This time, though, he wasn't alone.

'You might be thinking this is not what you expected. Don't worry, we are here just to monitor the activities. As I told you before, our Norman Security team will be arriving shortly. Then they will take over. I don't want them to be left grappling the situation alone,' he said uncertainly.

When the clocks struck 3.30 p.m., two men in matching blue T-shirts, with NASSO IT conference and Norman Cyber Security logos printed on them, entered through the sliding door. They went straight to the front desk, where they presented their documents. But instead of getting a go-ahead, they were soon surrounded by several hotel staff.

From a distance Kanu could see the problem faced by his Norman Cyber Security representatives. He took a deep breath, picked up his laptop bag and stood up.

Darshu looked at him, alarmed.

'Should I come?' she asked.

'No, it's okay. These guys may have forgotten to bring their papers. I think there's some confusion. I'll come back in a minute,' Kanu said.

Darshu held her breath and looked straight at the hotel entrance, as if searching for an exit. She saw a man with curly hair, wearing worn-out jeans and an old sweater, coming in through the sliding door. He held a large, yellow envelope in his hand and walked quickly. Soon, he reached the front desk, not far away from the counter where Kanu stood pretending to write something.

'Hi,' the man with curly hair started in a low voice. 'I'm here to meet Mr Samba Rajput. I believe he has checked in this morning.'

'Sorry sir, we've received very clear instructions not to entertain any request for Mr Samba,' the lady at reception replied.

But the man with curly hair was not convinced. 'Not to entertain? What rubbish? I'm Ranjit Bhardwaj of Nav Hindustan Group,' he barked. 'You think I'm here trying to invade the privacy of your client? Listen madam, your client is my business partner. Look here, this is the proposal for the Hyderabad Now Metro project.' Ranjit pointed to the yellow envelope in his hand. 'I want to know who your manager is this very instant!'

'Please sir, try to understand. We are only obeying orders. If you want the manager's number, I can provide you that. In fact, I'll call him right now,' the lady said nervously. 'But please understand, we have clear instructions about our VIP guests.'

Ranjit was now shifting his weight from one leg to the other in a menacing way. 'Okay, can you get me his secretary, Sheena? She must be on your guest list for sure.'

The receptionist clicked on the mouse below to check computer entries.

'Would you like to talk to her?' she asked.

'Yes,' Ranjit replied.

The lady connected the call and passed on the receiver to Ranjit. 'Sir, Ms Sheena is on the line,' the receptionist said.

'Sheena, this is Ranjit Bhardwaj of Nav Hindustan Group. I'm in the lobby. I thought I'd meet Samba at the hotel itself and discuss our VEMAYHTAS proposal for the Hyderabad Now Metro project. You know how it is with telephone lines. You never know who else is listening. And we can't send e-mails as well. Can you check with Samba if he can meet me now?'

Ranjit handed back the receiver to the receptionist without a word. Kanu glanced up while pretending to read a brochure, as Ranjit walked away in silence. Less than three metres away, Kanu could overhear the conversation between the representatives of Norman Cyber Security and the hotel staff.

One of the men clad in a blue Norman T-shirt was persistent in his pitch. 'Sir, when you shift your infrastructure, the servers are open for hackers to exploit the vulnerabilities. The entire hotel infrastructure becomes less secure,' he said. 'We have seen computers being targeted in a run-up to the annual summit of the Pharmacy Conclave in Mumbai. The hotel management did not reveal which companies were targeted but if you Google it, you will find many trade secrets were stolen during the conference. It was widely reported in the newspapers.'

'Okay, we'll check with our management about installing your software,' the hotel staff said doubtfully.

As the incident played out, Kanu decided not to get involved. Instead, he walked back to Darshu, pulled out his laptop and searched for information on Nav Hindustan Group, VEMAYHTAS and Hyderabad Now Metro.

The search results confirmed his doubts.

VEMAYHTAS had been listed as one of the consortium partners under Nav Hindustan Group that had bid for Hyderabad Now Metro. Why would Ranjit be so worried about his phone being tapped? Maybe Rana was using him as a proxy to accomplish his goals.

He thought back to the day he met his brother, Bala.

What was Bala trying to say? Only Sathyamev can kill Sathyamev. Did he mean that VEMAYHTAS could kill Sathyamev?

Kanu could feel it happening, a sudden euphoria taking over. He had pieced together the answer that had eluded him all these years. *Yes, that's it! VEMAYHTAS can cancel SATHYAMEV out!*

Convinced of the mightiest weapon in his hands, he signalled Darshu with a thumbs-up sign. 'We're done for the day,' he said. 'Come, let's go back to our hotel.'

EIGHTEEN

5 January–12 July 2008

A special contingent of armed men in camouflage uniforms, bulletproof vests and helmets knocked violently on the door of B-402 at Gulmohar Taj. It was a clandestine operation commissioned by the Hyderabad CID unit. Their target was Kanu Vasukumar, the illegal computer network leader, wanted for manipulating the stock markets through unlawful insider trading.

'Open the door,' screamed the group commander. 'This is a CID raid.'

There was no response.

The commander repeated himself. 'Open the door, this is a CID raid. If you don't open it now, we will have to break it open.'

Silence.

Looking at the hotel attendant, who was ducking behind the other men in uniform, the commander asked in a low voice, 'Are you sure they are still inside?'

'Yes, they haven't moved out,' replied the attendant.

'Okay then, listen, very silently open the door with your master key and move out immediately.'

The attendant did exactly as instructed.

Within seconds, the commander and the other uniformed men stormed the room.

'They are not inside,' yelled a man from inside the washroom.

By this time, another man had thrown open a window only to see more men in camouflage uniforms outside.

'They must have escaped through this window. Keep an eye on the vehicles outside,' said the man.

'Search inside the cabinets. They may have left something,' said the commander.

'There's a CD in the cupboard. It says: *For Rana*,' came a voice from behind.

'Get it. Let's check the other rooms.'

'What? He escaped again?' Rana screamed. 'Do you know how irresponsible that sounds?' He paced the length of the hotel. 'We cannot let him remain in the open. You understand?'

'We were this close to nabbing him.' Samba shook his head. 'Don't know if we should have hired our own men instead of relying on the state machinery.'

Rana's anger was not reflected in his voice when he spoke again.

'Do we have any idea where he could be right now?'

'I checked. He has not left Pune yet,' Samba said in a low voice. 'But he did leave something behind for you – a CD.' Samba flashed the disc. 'They found it in Kanu's room during the raid.'

'Did you check it?'

'No.'

'Fine, play it.'

Samba's hand trembled as he inserted the disc into the laptop. Kanu's face appeared on the screen: *I always wanted to hear that voice of yours, Uncle. Unfortunately, you keep changing your numbers. Here is mine: 8102777201.*

Suddenly, the screen turned black. It seemed Kanu had shot the video himself and had kept the message short.

'This is it? This is what he wanted to say?' said Rana, looking agitated. 'And now he wants me to call him. He doesn't know who I am yet.'

'I think we should call him. This could be a good opportunity to trace his location. We'll get to know exactly where he is right now. This time he won't escape.'

'Fine, get our men to finish off this task,' Rana said.

That evening, Kanu was driving through a deserted valley towards Lonavala, past the scenic forest of Khandala, when his cell phone buzzed. The number on display seemed unusual. It had the prefix showing +001 instead of the usual +91. Kanu wasn't sure who was on the other end of the call, but he could guess: Rana.

He felt a familiar aversion rise within him.

'Darshu, could you please answer the call?' Kanu said.

'Whose call is it?' she asked.

'Rana's.'

'Rana?' gasped Darshu, looking at the flashing device.

'Yeah, all you have to do is say *hello*, and turn it over to me. I will pull over in a minute,' said Kanu, looking in the rear-view mirror.

Darshu nodded and clicked the green button. Her prompt response to the voice at the other end was simple. 'Could you please hold the line while I hand over the phone to Kanu?' she said.

Then she looked at Kanu and pointed to the phone.

'He sounds angry,' she mouthed.

Kanu smiled wryly. He had known all along that a conversation with his uncle was inevitable. And that it wasn't going to be a pleasant one whenever it happened.

'Sorry, that was my girlfriend,' he started without listening to the voice. 'She was playing with my cell when your call came. Who am I talking to?'

'Your days are numbered, Kanu. How long do you think you can keep hiding like a rat?' Rana's voice thundered. 'You were lucky to escape from the CID. Had they caught you for tripping the stock market, you could have gotten away with a jail term or even less. The penalty you will now pay for disrupting my business is –'

'Your business? Who says it's your business?' Kanu cut him short. 'I know you're hurting, uncle. But that's not your fault. I'm surprised how you do business without having any knowledge of it. Do you always bribe people into doing things your way?'

'You think I bribe people? I buy them. I rule the business.'

'You think you'll buy the Hyderabad Now Metro project as well? No. I'll never let that happen. This time you lose.' Kanu smiled again. 'I'll make sure that the Navarjuna Group makes it to the winners list. Good luck.'

Back in the hotel room, Rana had one final bit of advice – warning, really – for Kanu, but he was left holding a dead line. 'Listen – hello – hello –' Rana screamed into the headset. The emptiness of the disconnected line rattled in his ears. For several seconds he stood in stunned silence.

Rana then picked up the CD with *For Rana* written on it and walked to the other end of hotel room where a few technicians, under the guidance of Samba, were working on their computers.

'Samba, did you get his location?' Rana said.

'Yes, he's somewhere on the Pune–Mumbai highway – the old route. I've sent all our men to get him,' Samba said.

'Clean it up this time. He should not be in a position to send another disc like this.' Rana waved the one in his hand. 'Also, check with our IT forensic guy to see if there's any hidden malware in this CD. The laptop on which you played the video, isolate it and make sure to format it. I don't want to take any risks this time.'

Samba nodded and was on his way towards the door when Rana interrupted him again.

'One more thing. Ask Ranjit and Chingappa to meet me in an hour. I want to discuss the progress of the Hyderabad Now Metro project,' he said.

Along the Sahyadri mountain range, Kanu steered his car towards the garrison town of Lonavala. As his vehicle cut through the busy traffic, Darshu could see men in blue uniform stopping vehicles ahead of them.

'Fantastic,' she murmured as the vehicle came to a standstill. 'Now we stay in this car while they track us down. I told you we should have continued to Mumbai.'

'Look here,' Kanu said, 'there's nothing to be afraid of. This area is under navy jurisdiction.' He pulled out an ID card with the Indian Navy signage on it. 'I'm authorized to enter this campus. Most people here know me by my name.'

'Okay?'

'You don't believe me? There's a navy technical institute about 800 metres to the left. I've been helping them gather counter-intelligence information from our neighbouring countries. Here, this badge is only for a privileged few.'

'Wow! And how did you get in touch with the navy?'

'Ah, there's an ongoing programme to dig out information from the dark net. And we are also building our cyber-attack capabilities. It's a long story, will tell you some other time.'

'And I thought that your work was mostly about hacking the stock market – and attending uninvited business conferences – and getting into trouble.'

'Very funny,' smiled Kanu.

That evening, Samba stood near the sitting area of his luxurious suite and gestured at his guests to sit. His visitors, Chingappa Sampath and Ranjit Bhardwaj, each a millionaire in his own right, were front men for VEMAYHTAS' ambitious new project Hyderabad Now Metro.

Chingappa was tall and lean, in his mid-fifties, with wavy black hair. He had served as finance secretary to the current chief minister before being shifted to the public welfare ministry and was considered the most influential dealmaker in the corridors of power.

Rana looked at Chingappa for a moment.

'Chingappa, you've been – what do they call it – unreachable these days. How are we supposed to carry out our business with your CM if you are not interested?' Rana said.

Chingappa gave no reply. He simply looked back at Rana.

Ranjit, sitting beside Chingappa on the couch, cleared his throat and looked at Samba standing several feet away. 'I came here today with this document,' Ranjit said, looking at the yellow envelope with the Nav Hindustan logo on it. 'It contains all the leaked memos that the project director gave me.'

Ranjit tossed the envelope on the coffee table and looked into Rana's eyes. 'We at Nav Hindustan will do whatever you say. Everything.'

Rana didn't bother to look at the envelope or the table. 'Tell me, Ranjit, what would it take for the Navarjuna Group to win the metro contract? I'm not concerned about what the director says; I'm more concerned about the Navarjuna Group.'

Again, there was silence. Rana's eyes narrowed.

'Ranjit, I'm expecting an answer.'

'There are rumours that the Navarjuna Group's chairman is sweetening the deal,' Ranjit began hesitantly. 'He is making lucrative offers to our chief minister's son-in-law.'

'Great! Now it's a son-in-law,' Samba exclaimed. 'These politicians just can't keep from begging.' He walked over to the couch and stood behind Chingappa, resting his hands on the visitor's shoulders. 'How many sons and daughters does this man have? No, seriously? First, it was a son. Now, it's a son-in-law,' Samba said mockingly.

Chingappa finally mustered up enough courage to speak. 'Sir, it's not like that. Yes, someone told me the Navarjuna Group is planning to start a religious channel for the CM's son-in-law. But it's not confirmed. Let me tell you, our technical bid for the project was well received. Now we are competing against the four pre-qualified consortia for the contract. It all depends on the financial bids,' he said. 'Last I met the chief minister, he was confident of our offer. But, yes, they are expecting some big rewards in return.'

'I'm sure they know we'll not disappoint them,' Rana said.

'We will be happy to make our CM even richer,' Samba joined in.

'Sir, it all goes to the party fund,' replied Chingappa.

'We are deviating from the topic,' Rana said. He straightened and looked at Chingappa squarely. 'Now tell me, Chingappa, we have a consortium partner from Thailand. And the Navarjuna Group has tied up with the German firm –'

'Symons.'

'Yes. My only concern is the technical points we lost in the overall assessment. How much more do we have to pay in our financial bid to compensate the lost points?'

Chingappa felt sweat break out on his forehead as he considered the question. He knew that a wrong answer would paralyse his future forever.

'The chief minster is on our side. There's nothing to worry about on that front,' he reassured Rana. 'Now it all depends on the financial bids. How much more should we bid for? I can't say that now, sir. But please, let me tell you again, the chief minister is on our side.'

'Okay, that's encouraging. Then there are other bidders. Those guys are also on good terms with the CM. Is there any way we could get information on their bids from the inside? That way we could be assured of the contract even before the bids are opened,' Rana said.

'Yes, our competitor has acquired an impressive set of technology but then, there will be only one winner. And that would be us,' Chingappa said.

Rana nodded, now growing a little more confident. 'Chingappa, I want you to tell me what these competitors are up to. We cannot afford to lose out on any information. If the son-in-law also wants his religious channel, I'm willing to finance it. But tell me, Chingappa, what's the current position of the government? Why aren't they announcing the deadlines for submission of the financial bids?'

'It's the biggest metro rail project *ever* to be undertaken in the public-private partnership mode, sir. The state governments and the Centre are providing a grant of Rs 4,000 crore as viability-gap funding. Who wouldn't want a 4,000-crore largesse from the government? There are so many interested people visiting the CM these days. What can I say?'

'That's not the only reason why we don't want to let go of the project, am I right, Ranjit?' Rana said.

Ranjit leaned forward to pull out papers from the envelope he had tossed on the table minutes before. 'More than that, it's the land bank in the offering that's making people visit the chief minister's office. As I see it, the build, operate and transfer, or BOT, model is not very complicated. What this means is we *build*, we *operate*, and the government *transfers* the land to us. This map has all the details. Look at all the major depots in red dots,' said Ranjit, pointing to the map on the table. 'All this will be built on the government land. There's 99 acres in Miyapur, 77 acres in Habsiguda and 17 acres in Falaknuma. Then there's 12 acres in Gymkhana Grounds, Parade Grounds and Jubilee Bus Station. In all, we get 492 acres of prime land. Then there are 63 rail stations and terminals, all at the prime locations. In thirty years, this project has potential to make anyone richer than the Nizams.'

Rana stood up, clutching the papers that Ranjit held. 'Yes, this project can make anyone richer than the Nizams.'

Then he smiled, a rare glint of happiness visible in his eyes.

When viewed on Google Maps, the Hyderabad Now Metro seemed to be taking a peculiar route to reach territories that were linked to huge tracts of empty land with no particular significance. Kanu studied the narrow strip of the rail route that connected Shilparamam and Nagole with a proposed plan for future extension in both directions.

'Look at this, Darshu,' Kanu said. 'If you are a true investigative journalist, this might interest you.'

Not far away, sipping her coffee inside the cozy guest cottage, Darshu mischievously eyed him over the brim of the cup. 'Investigative? Who said I'm an investigative journalist?' she said.

'Come here, take a look at this.'

Darshu walked over to him. 'I guess you'll never leave your laptop. Ever.'

'Never,' he said. Then he keyed in more text in the search bar of the map. 'This portion of barren land you see, this is where they have proposed to stretch the existing line. Forget that, look at this brown area,' Kanu said pointing to a small patch on the monitor. 'This is where they are taking the metro in the second phase. If the price of this land today is, say, Rs 1,200 per square foot, it will jump to Rs 15,000 just like that. And you might think, whose property is this, right? Well, these are all benami properties.'

'Rana is bidding under VEMAYHTAS, isn't he?'

'Yup, on the surface of it, this looks like just another project. But look closer and you will see inaccuracies at every level. I was doing some study. It's a rock-strewn landscape, so it's almost impossible for the metro to take an underground route. So what will they do? They will deconstruct existing structures, monuments, everything else. Second, there's an existing rapid transit system in the form of MMTS, connecting all major portions of the city. So now what will they do? They will reduce the number of trips, start operating these trains at odd times and then they will stop all feeder services. Which means, even if a passenger reaches the station, there will be no auto rickshaw, no buses around.'

'That's very inventive, politically!'

'Yes, politically inventive it is! Now, this article from an IIM professor is very suggestive. He says that the state could have opted for monorail systems, which has potential benefits in crowded, high-density areas. But the project cost was less; less cost, less profit, less bribe money. It's all simple maths. Then, he says, by developing dedicated bus lanes and pothole-free roads, the state can improve the infrastructure at a fraction of the cost of this project. The fraction here is 0.5 per cent. But the government will never do that because there's no money to be made in potholes. Wow!'

'Hmm, it's purely a vehicle to make rich people richer.'

'And more powerful,' Kanu added.

'So what are you planning?'

'Me? It's your work. You are the PR rep. It's your job to create good stories about Rana's competitors.'

'And why would I do that?' she asked.

'To vacuum up Rana's money. You can make millions from his fall,' Kanu said.

Later that evening, Kanu sat in silence, staring intensely at the screen. While operating in cyberspace, he had the ability to move godlike through databases, get access to stashed passwords and read private messages. But on this day, he couldn't find anything on Nav Hindustan Group or the VEMAYHTAS proposal for the metro project. *Rana is being very careful this time*, he thought. *He must be keeping all his documents offline.*

But then there were other partners in the consortium.

Kanu was soon browsing through the internal memos of the Navarjuna Group. In two hours, he had downloaded every possible piece of information available on their private systems and networks, including the technical white paper on the metro project.

One topic in particular, recurring in several internal memos, interested him enough to do a background check. Navarjuna management had been searching for a liaison officer, somebody who could lobby in the government offices.

'Darshu?' Kanu called out.

'What?' Darshu shouted back from the other room.

'Listen, have you ever tried doing a story on Navarjuna before?'

'Navarjuna Group of Pune?'

'Yes. They've shifted their HQ to Delhi. It's not Pune any more.'

'No, didn't. Why do you ask?'

'They are looking for a liaison officer. You could apply.'

'No, thank you very much.'

'No, seriously. You could apply on behalf of our PR agency,' he said.

Kanu picked up his laptop and walked over to the other room. She was sitting on a wooden chair, immersed in her own computer. He sat on the edge of the bed looking at her. 'Navarjuna Group always keeps a low-key profile. There are hardly any interviews with the press. And the ones that have appeared are short pieces tucked away in the business pages. Someone has to help them get good press.'

'You do that,' she said with a smirk and went back to her laptop.

'But it's your work.'

'Then, can you do that for me please?' she said.

Kanu kept staring at her in disbelief.

'Okay, if you want me to get rid of my laptop, you've got to get rid of yours first.'

'Done.' She slammed the lid of the laptop shut.

Kanu spent the next few hours modelling the Biz-Bazzar PR website after the world's leading PR agency. He had linked the functions of the dummy site in such a way that it became the de-facto Indian subsidiary of an international giant.

Then he snooped into the mailbox of a certain Patrick Gray of Symons, the consortium partner of Navarjuna. Using Patrick's account, Kanu then wrote an e-mail to the HR manager of the Navarjuna Group.

In his mail, Patrick highlighted the good work of Biz-Bazzar PR and recommended the work handled by their parent company in Germany.

Within a few days, after several rounds of telephonic discussion, a business meeting was set up between the Biz-Bazzar PR team and the Navarjuna corporate communication team in Delhi. The agenda: getting good press.

Later that week, when Darshu met the Navarjuna Group management and corporate communication team, with Kanu in tow, in a cramped conference room in Delhi, her mission was simple. She had to cut through the news clutter and start a debate about the company's effective partnership with Symons to get good press. She succeeded beyond anything the Navarjuna team or even Kanu had ever imagined. Her contact list of journalists as friends, her idea of creating metro-rail employment drives in colleges, utilization of Web 2.0 and inserting specially authored columns resonated hugely with the Navarjuna team. In addition, the yearly retention fees quoted by Biz-Bazzar PR agency was less than the annual salary of an executive working in their office.

As expected, Biz-Bazzar PR bagged the contract.

The immediate task assigned to the agency was creating positive stories. In turn, the Navarjuna team promised to cooperate and provide leads on all their activities related to the Hyderabad Now Metro project.

A week later, news stories on the Hyderabad Now Metro started trickling in to the *Afternoon Times, Deccan Courier,* the *Express of Hyderabad* and other dailies. Mysteriously, somebody had leaked every sordid detail of the Hyderabad Now Metro project management since its inception and the way the bidding process was flawed, favouring the least technically qualified consortium of VEMAYHTAS and Nav Hindustan Group.

At the same time, a fierce debate raged among policy makers and engineers on a popular community board, skyscrappercity.co.in. The argument was on the merits of the Navarjuna Group as being the most capable engineering firm against the ill-qualified partnership VEMAYHTAS had cobbled together. The discussion, however, was indirectly moderated by Kanu, who had surreptitiously gained administrative rights.

In another threaded discussion forum – hyderabadcitybulletin.in – initiated by a devoted group of infrastructure professionals, an anonymous user had posted several confidential and genuine-looking documents detailing the Navarjuna Group's financial bid document. Rumours abounded. It seemed almost certain that the consortium led by VEMAYHTAS and the Nav Hindustan Group would never make it to the winning list, despite getting a back-door entry in the first round of the bidding process.

NINETEEN

5 January–19 July 2008

'That security guard controlling our entrance gate has everything to keep this place safe. Guns, night goggles, reinforcement, police support – everything. But he cannot stop incessant attack on this office,' Rana said, as he turned away from the window of his penthouse to walk back to his desk. The computer monitor on his desk displayed video feeds from all the security cameras. A security man with a rifle in his hands sitting in a small, wooden cabin at the entrance could be seen in a tiny grid among several moving images.

Samba sat on the couch a few feet away, looking unsure. 'I understand – I understand what you are trying to say …' Samba began, but couldn't think of anything more to say.

Rana stared for a long time at the image of the guard with the rifle. 'How do you expect this man to protect Sathyamev? He doesn't even know we're under attack. We have to build a stronger fort, but are we lobbying hard enough for the metro project? No, we are not. Are we getting good press? No, we are not. Are we spending money? Hell, we are spending to the hilt. We're leaking so much money I had to pledge almost half my holdings,' Rana said through clenched teeth.

Rana's outburst was not unfounded. If the news report published in the *Express of Hyderabad* was to be believed, the Navarjuna Group had set aside thousands of crores of rupees just to finance the Hyderabad Now Metro project.

Samba leaned forward, this time paying attention. 'To begin with, the bidding process is structured in such a way that we will get all the information. But we don't have any control over our competitors, do we?'

All these years Samba had done everything exactly as Rana had wanted, and now, as the final dates for submission of the financial bids neared, he was growing disheartened by his brother's hasty assessments. 'Chingappa still maintains we will win the bid. If you want, I can get in touch with the CM's secretary, Jagjivan. He's also on our rolls,' Samba said.

'You just don't get it. There's smoke. There's fire. All of it can't be a rumour. There has to be some grain of truth in the news.' Rana flipped through the newspaper on his desk and picked up a pen to underline an article with the headline: *Navarjuna arms itself with 2000 crores for Hyderabad Now Metro*.

Rana sat down cross-legged, holding the newspaper. 'I tell you, these politicians and bureaucrats can't be trusted. They'll take money from everyone and we won't even know about it. Do you understand the implications of losing this bid? All our investment in real estate? Nothing. All our money spent on politicians and their relatives? Nothing. And worst of all? We go back to adding *zeros and ones.* No matter what it takes – we must be in a position where we can defend ourselves.'

'I understand –'

Darshu walked with a tray of coffee in her hand, unmindful of the other passengers staring at her. Not far away, Kanu sat in the waiting area at the New Delhi airport in Palam, his eyes glued to the monitor of his laptop.

As Darshu took a seat, Kanu glanced at her for a second and then went back to tapping his fingers on the keyboard. Darshu carefully wrapped the coffee cup in tissue paper and offered it to him.

'Coffee?' she asked.

He nodded without looking at her. Then he stopped typing and looked at her, smiling. 'Thank you,' he said. After taking the coffee, he set it down on an empty chair next to him. His gaze immediately shifted back to the laptop screen.

Darshu sighed, looking away.

As she sat there sipping her coffee, the low sunlight flooded the room, cutting through the ambient lights of the airport terminal. She had always wanted to make her first international trip memorable.

'Morning sun – serene weather – drizzle – such a nice time to be outside,' she said sipping her coffee.

Kanu didn't respond.

She tapped him gently on the shoulder. 'I'll never know if they brew coffee so well here at the airport or the coffee just tastes so good in anticipation of a long journey.'

'What?' He came out of his haze of thoughts.

'Nothing. Forget it.' She looked away, saddened.

Kanu sipped his coffee, then leaned back looking at her, this time with genuine interest. 'The coffee here is good. And there's this journey factor as well. I think it's both.'

Darshu smiled. She knew his work was important.

She got up to toss the empty cup into a bin. While coming back, she picked up a newspaper from a stand nearby and began leafing through it.

'Hmm, this story will interest you,' she said.

'What is it?'

'I haven't read it completely. Here, you read it.'

Kanu picked up the paper and began to read the article:

Hike in grants for Hyderabad Now Metro

The Centre is about to increase primary grant levels for the upcoming Hyderabad Now Metro project from 20 per cent to 30 per cent.

The urban development minister told reporters that a decision would be taken in a few days, before the last date of submission of the financial bids is finalized.

```
The Central grant to the Rs 10,000-crore
Hyderabad Now Metro project would increase
by over Rs 3,000 crore.
```

As usual, Kanu wasn't the least surprised. 'It says the winner of this bid will now receive as much as 5,000 crores. That's 3,000 crores from the Centre and 2,000 from the state.'

'But it all depends on the bid amount, doesn't it?'

'That's correct. But the bid amount would in turn depend on the competitors. Now, if Navarjuna were to bid a large amount, others would be forced to follow suit. Such claims would require more convincing evidence. Something positive. It doesn't have to be true, but it has to appear like the truth.'

'You mean propaganda?'

'Yes.'

'Is that what you are doing over there?' she asked, pointing to his laptop.

'*Exactly.*'

'Good. Want a bite? I'm already feeling hungry. Tell me, what kind of food do they serve? I mean, this is a first-class ticket. Do they serve wine as well?'

'I guess.'

'But I don't drink.'

'Then pass it on to me.'

'What if you got drunk in the flight?'

'You look nervous –'

'No, I'm fine – sort of ...'

'It's all very simple. We'll have a meeting with World Bank International officials. The meeting date, time, venue, everything is fixed. Think of it as a paid holiday. A paid holiday, for as long as you want.'

'Tell me, is this your first trip to Singapore?'

'As a Sathyamev employee? Yes!' he said.

At 1.10 p.m. on 12 July 2008, Samba's gaze was fixed on a cheap, disposable cell phone that lit up in his hand. The device displayed an unknown incoming number and made no sound. But Samba had been expecting this call. He punched the green button and held it to his ear.

'Chingappa? What's the latest?'

As Samba listened to the voice at the other end, his face turned bright red, beads of sweat forming on his forehead. 'That's not good,' he muttered. 'What can be done now?' He shook his head in disagreement. 'No, we can't fix this unless we get a green signal. I'll let you know immediately.'

Samba disconnected the line, then picked up a yellow envelope from the table below and stood up. 'It is confirmed. Navarjuna Group is quoting a negative grant of 1,200 crores,' he said.

Rana was at his desk, keenly observing his computer screen that displayed rail routes crisscrossing the city of Hyderabad. He pretended to be unaware of Samba's conversation on the phone.

'Who was that?' Rana said.

'Chingappa. His information is coming from the law firm that's assigned to vet all correspondence from the bidders. We have less than an hour to submit our revised bid,' Samba said.

'How much did you say Navarjuna Group –'

'Twelve hundred crores. Instead of seeking subsidy from the government, these morons are offering 1,200 crores to emerge as the lowest bidder. And they have also committed a revenue of 30,000 crores over the project's period of thirty years. It's madness.'

'So the rumour was right after all.'

'It seems so.'

'Can you connect the line again?' Rana asked.

Samba punched the green button on the device and handed it over to Rana.

'Chingappa, is it true that Navarjuna is quoting a negative grant?' Rana paused to listen. 'Twelve hundred crores is worth investing in. Don't worry, I'll get you our fresh bid in about thirty minutes.' He disconnected.

Rana stood up and began pacing the room. 'We'll make a counter offer. Our bid amount would be 1,250 crores. And we will commit 30,300 crores for the project period of thirty years. Open up that envelope.'

The yellow envelope Samba carried was thick and heavy. It had 'Hyderabad Now Metro proposal' written on it in block letters.

'Should I ask Sheena to get a new print?' Samba asked.

'No, we must do it ourselves,' Rana said.

TWENTY

20–21 July 2008

On 20 July 2008, crew from all major television networks camped in the front lawn of the Hyderabad Now Metro office, each vying to be the first to break the news. As everyone waited for an official announcement, one reporter, in her recognizable black turtleneck and a red long coat, was readying herself, microphone in hand.

She looked into the camera, took a deep breath and began her story: 'I'm here outside the Hyderabad Now Metro building. In about half an hour, government officials will make a formal announcement to declare the winning group or consortium that will bag the prestigious project. As per the protocol, the director will open the sealed bid submitted by all four consortia for this Rs 10,000-crore project. The consortium with the lowest bid will be declared the winner. The representative of the winning consortium will then be required to deposit the money to conclude the procedure. We will keep you informed of the developments throughout the day, but before that, let's take a very short commercial break –'

Thousands of miles away in Singapore, Kanu leaned forward to grab the remote control and flip the news channel streaming live images from Hyderabad. On the screen, the female reporter in a black turtleneck and a long red coat gave way to a reporter clad in a crisp blue shirt who reported live from the Hyderabad Now Metro premises.

The reporter glanced at his notes before looking into the camera: 'Remember, the Hyderabad Now Metro project is India's biggest metro project involving construction of 71 km of elevated metro rail that will crisscross the city of Hyderabad. The metro executive team is now locked away making their decision, which we can expect at 11.30 a.m. There are unconfirmed reports that the VEMAYHTAS-led consortium will bag the project, due to massive financial backing of Sathyamev Computers. But let me remind you, this is an unconfirmed report from our sources –'

Kanu lay on an easy chair, staring at the television affixed to the wall of the room. 'They're already picking up the leaked news,' he said as he lowered the volume. 'We now have to wait for the final verdict. It's like a ticking time bomb.'

Darshu wrapped herself in a blanket and snuggled more deeply into the bed. 'What if the ticking time bomb doesn't explode?' she asked, wary of the game Kanu was playing.

'Hmm, that was the wrong analogy. It's more like a game of chess. Even if Rana escapes this time, he won't in the days to come. Let's wait,' he said.

Back in Hyderabad, Ranjit Bhardwaj stared at the giant television screen playing a special story on NewsReview TV channel. A man wearing a dark blue suit and a matching tie coordinated the discussion: 'Of course, the metro officials have been cautious in their statement. But is there any information as to who the front-runner is?'

The scene shifted to the exterior of the Hyderabad Now Metro building, with the voice of a reporter taking over: 'All indications are that the process of evaluation went smoothly. What's happening right now inside the closed doors will be known soon. But if the stock market is any indicator, Nav Hindustan Group shares witnessed about 9.5 per cent rise at the Mumbai stock exchange. The company officials have not yet confirmed the news but –'

As the reporter was about to finish the sentence, the camera abruptly cut back to the news anchor: 'Just hold on there, Bopanna, we're getting news from the metro officials now. This is breaking news, exclusive on our channel. The VEMAYHTAS-led consortium has been selected as the Hyderabad Now Metro developer for the city. The consortium emerged as the lowest bidder when the financial bids were opened. We are getting reports that VEMAYHTAS consortium has offered to pay Rs

1,250 crore. In addition to this, they have offered Rs 30,300 crore across the thirty-year contract period as royalty to the government. They will not take a single slice of government grant, which was available under the viability gap funding.

'Though there was a provision for seeking viability gap funding under the norms of the public-private partnership, VEMAYHTAS had agreed to pay Rs 30,300 crore as reverse grant to the government over a period of thirty years. While three of the bidders sought financial commitments from the government in the form of venture gap funding, VEMAYHTAS offered to pay back the government and refused to take any grant.

'The Reliant Group consortium asked for a subsidy from the government of Rs 3,100 crore, while Navarjuna Group wanted Rs 1,200 crore. But VEMAYHTAS offered to pay the government 1,250 crores.'

Ranjit at once pulled out his cell phone and dialled Samba's number.

'Samba, sir, I just saw the – hello – hello –' Ranjit stammered. 'I understand – I know you must be busy –' Ranjit stared at his cell phone as the line got disconnected.

'Where in hell is Chingappa? Find him,' Rana barked aloud, his voice reverberating in the small guest room of the Hyderabad Now Metro office. Rana and Samba were especially invited to the metro building by the director to witness the bidding process.

Samba swallowed hard, making an effort to speak. 'He called – he was here during the bidding process.' Samba's face was bleak. 'He was afraid –'

'Where the hell is he now?'

'He called, he said he is sorry for the mistake. He said he read the quote from the original copy of the proposal. He still maintains that the Navarjuna bid amount was a negative grant of Rs 1,200 crore.'

'So what the hell happened? The figures changed all on their own? I want him now. Call my bodyguards.'

Samba stood stunned, staring at his cellphone. He pressed a speed dial number without thinking. Even before he could disconnect the call, SISI Security members were inside the guest room.

Rana looked at the armed men. 'Get me Chingappa. Even if he is hiding in a hole, I want him,' Rana's voice thundered. 'You know what is to be done if he resists. You can go now,' Rana said.

After the SISI men were gone, Rana continued angrily, 'When is the CM's secretary coming?'

'Any moment now. I called up our lawyer as well. He will be arriving shortly. The meeting is arranged in the conference room.'

'Get me a printed copy of the Navarjuna bid.'

'I'm trying,' Samba said.

Minutes later, Samba showed Rana into a dingy conference room of the metro building. Seated around the table were two harassed-looking men, both in their mid-forties. Before the men could rise from their seats to congratulate Rana, he gestured for them to remain seated.

'This is not the right time to get me started,' Rana announced menacingly. 'You may not be smart enough to understand, but this is not how we wanted to win the bid.' Rana looked back over his shoulder. 'Samba, did you inform them why they are here?'

'Yes. Jagjivan Reddy will clarify all our doubts about the future of this project.'

The man with thick glasses and dyed brown hair smiled. As the principal secretary of the chief minister, Reddy had played a vital role in tweaking government processes to help Rana procure lucrative deals.

Samba looked at the other man. 'Pushkar will help us understand the legal aspects of the deal.'

'Good. Tell me, Pushkar, what could happen if we pulled out of this agreement, citing some problem?' Rana asked.

Reddy cleared his throat. 'That's not possible. You cannot pull out, Rana. We have put in months – years, in fact – just to ensure that this contract can be yours. You can't pull out now.'

'I know. I don't want to lose this project either. But I still want to know the consequences of us pulling out.'

Everyone in the room stared at the lawyer.

'The deposit money of Rs 100 crore would be forfeited. Plus, VEMAYHTAS would be ineligible for any government project in the future. In fact, VEMAYHTAS could be blacklisted for defaulting on its promises. All our existing projects with the government, including stalled projects such as the Krishnapatu port, could be withdrawn or terminated,' Pushkar said.

'Rana, don't worry. The land we helped you procure on the outskirts can fetch you ten times the amount you have bid for. It's not a bad bid to win. Three years from now, this will start reaping dividends,' Reddy assured him.

'True. As I said, I don't want to lose this project. But did you see the television report? They're all after me. Sathyamev's shares are down by more than 12 per cent. They think that I have committed a sin by investing Sathyamev's money into VEMAYHTAS,' Rana said.

'Yeah, I saw the news and commotion over the bid amount –' Reddy said.

'So what do we do now?' Samba asked.

'I think, it's better if we wait for this to die down. The future is safe,' Reddy replied.

'Stupid stockbrokers. They are trying to force their views on me. Those people, they don't realize that it's my business. I'm the one who dishes out crumbs to them. And I'm the one who will decide their fate,' Rana said.

The room went silent.

Reddy stood up. 'I'm glad you called me here. But before I leave, tell me Rana, what made you bid like this? I told you very clearly we were trying to get you 5,000 crores from the government funds. Instead you promised to give 1,250 crores *to* the government. What made you think you were losing?'

Rana looked puzzled. He had no answer.

The ticker text scrolling at the bottom of a flat panel monitor that hung on the wall outside the studio of NewsReview TV network said it all. Breaking News: *VEMAYHTAS bags Hyderabad Now Metro project.* The sensational bid was big enough for the network to allocate an hour to discuss the matter with the panel.

Inside the studio at the anchor desk, Arvind Kumar was going through his notes when the red light flashed on. He began speaking: 'This one's a head-shaker. The Hyderabad Now Metro bidding process was never supposed to go like this. In fact, the result was so unexpected, government officials are scrambling because their bid documents had not even considered the possibility of the government being the net financial gainer. The state and the central government had expected to dole out about 50 per cent of the project cost, or Rs 5,000 crore, as a capital subsidy. But the opposite happened. I'm Arvind Kumar and you are watching NewsReview Prime Time. When we return we will talk with our experts about this episode and why Sathyamev shares are sliding.'

Arvind was in his element. His observation on the VEMAYHTAS project stood out in part because of his online research – mostly pulled out from skyscrappercity.co.in – and in part because of his confidence in the guest on the show.

As the commercial break came to an end, the camera pulled back to a wider angle, revealing an old man dressed in a dark gray suit. Arvind smiled, looking at the camera. 'Welcome back. Today we have Mr Shrinivasan NR, a technocrat who is hailed as the metro-man for his unflinching dedication to operationalize the Delhi Metro,' he said excitedly. 'It would be an understatement to say we are all proud of him. We're fortunate enough to have Mr Shrinivasan here to discuss the metro project in Hyderabad being awarded to VEMAYHTAS. Welcome to our studio, Mr Shrinivasan NR.'

The old man smiled and nodded. Arvind began with his questions.

'First off, what do you make of VEMAYHTAS being awarded this contract?'

Shrinivasan leaned forward, his elbows on the edge of the desk, his fingers together. 'As I see it, VEMAYHTAS has no prior experience of building any metro rail projects. Their consortium consist of Thai Rail. We all know how credible that sounds. To top that, now the VEMAYHTAS consortium is offering over 30,300 crore rupees to the state government for giving them an opportunity to build the 71 km metro project in the city. This in itself makes me feel there are other motives behind the project. But will the government step up and probe into why this ludicrous offer was accepted in the first place?'

Arvind looked on, waiting for his guest to finish. Then he began. 'I know, not many people understand why VEMAYHTAS bid for this huge amount. But then, it's the government that will benefit from this deal.'

Shrinivasan smiled. 'Let's not forget that the reckless bid of VEMAYHTAS has a self-serving aspect to it as well. VEMAYHTAS is believed to be looking at expanding the project on two routes, not just to make its bid viable but also to get more value for its properties by providing connectivity. Sathyamev, the parent company of VEMAYHTAS, owns thousands of acres on the city's outskirts. This land can be developed into mega residential and commercial ventures.'

'But Sathyamev's share prices are down. Last I checked, investors are not happy with Mr Rana Rajput's decision to invest in the metro project. In the USA, where the company is listed as well, the stock market has rejected their idea. What do you make of that?'

Shrinivasan smiled again. 'They *have* to reject this idea. Look, two wrongs do not make one right. If one wrong is committed, then another wrong can never cancel it out.'

On 21 July 2008, the security camera feeds at the famous Ship Hotel at Marina Bay in Singapore showed a man in a black shirt and grey sports coat with a suitcase walk into the coffee shop. The same person was later seen having a lively conversation with a man already seated in the crowded shop. For a few minutes the two chatted, and when the man in the grey sports coat walked out of the room, he had left behind his suitcase.

The man in the grey sports coat and the one seated in the coffee shop were not instantly identifiable, but it seemed obvious – even to those watching the live security camera feeds – that the two had a very different kind of business meeting.

Exactly five hours after that meeting in Singapore, Arvind Kumar heard a discreet beep announcing an incoming fax message at his NewsReview TV studio cabin. He walked over to the desk and drew out the copy, his eyes scanning the page.

It was a press release from the World Bank International bureau disclosing the debarment of Sathyamev from all its projects.

Sathyamev Computers Debarred for
EIGHT Years by World Bank International

21 July 2008, Singapore – World Bank International has terminated existing contracts and debarred Sathyamev Computers, one of India's largest software companies, for eight years. Following a forensic analysis, bank investigators discovered that one or more contractors from Sathyamev Computer Services had covertly installed spyware on workstations inside the bank's headquarters. The bank also believes that the firm is engaged in providing improper benefits to bank staff and is involved in a series of cyber break-ins to steal sensitive information.

Arvind put on his jacket and punched an intercom number. 'Hey, listen. I just received a fax from the World Bank International. Can you please check if it's genuine? If it's true, we are breaking this story. Ask our team to be prepared for a special session,' he said over the phone before rushing out of his studio.

Soon Arvind Kumar was back at the anchor's desk gazing at the camera when the red light flashed on. He began speaking: 'The biggest news of the day is coming from Singapore. If you thought the VEMAYHTAS investment of 30,300 crores was bad enough news for Sathyamev, you couldn't be more wrong. Today, World Bank International has issued a press release stating that it has terminated Sathyamev Computers' existing contract worth 500 million and debarred it for eight years.

'In the last two hours, Sathyamev's stock price on the New York stock exchange has lost 47 per cent. Meanwhile, our source tells us that the registrar of companies will initiate a probe into Sathyamev's investment in VEMAYHTAS.'

TWENTY-ONE

22 July 2008

The next day, just after 8.30 in the morning, Rana sat with his legs stretched out in front, his head leaning back against the sofa. He was in the waiting room of the chief minster's chamber, alone. The dramatic fall of Sathyamev's share prices in the international stock market – with fear of banks placing increasing demands on him to cover margin calls on his pledged stock – had forced his unexpected visit.

Rana sat there, his gaze directed to the ceiling, when a young staffer dressed in a blue half-sleeve apron and matching slacks approached him. He held a tray with a cup of steaming hot coffee on it. As he pushed aside the newspapers on the coffee table – all of which had Rana's photograph on the front page – the man couldn't hide his excitement.

'Sir, I saw you in the news yesterday,' he said. 'You looked very real on TV as well.'

Rana sat there, lost in his own incoherent world. 'When will Jagjivan – when is he coming? Jagjivan?' he asked wearily.

'They are all looking very busy.'

'They? You mean, the CM?'

'No, sir. We don't have access to the CM, sir. Jagjivan, sir, only makes all the arrangements. Right now, he is with some foreigners – some delegation?'

'Just inform Jagjivan that I want to meet the chief minister, urgently.'

'Sure sir,' he said.

As the man left, Rana stared at the portrait of the chief minister that hung over the entrance to his office. The crooked smile and intense stare were in sharp contrast to Rana's own failing composure.

A few minutes later when Jagjivan appeared from the same doorway, Rana stood up and came forward to shake hands.

'Thank god you came. I have been up all night making frantic calls,' Rana said.

'Yeah, I know, the news is very disturbing. I'm sorry I couldn't take your calls yesterday. You know how it is with the election season. At night I have to power-off my phone.'

'Yeah, I know.'

'Tell me, what brings you here so unexpectedly?'

'I think you know. We paid the balance of the money for the metro project, but now there's a cash-flow problem. The stock market is collapsing. Today, when the market opens, banks will start demanding money to cover margin calls on my pledged shares. There's no way I can stop this crisis from deepening any further. There's only one option ...'

'What can we do, tell me?'

'I can't borrow from the market or the banks. There's no time available. My only hope is the chief minster. He can help me get corporate loans or guarantees against the metro deal. Otherwise, I can't cover these impending margin calls. Remember, you said the state will guarantee to pay back the money that was invested in the metro.'

'Yes, I remember that. But we offered you close to 5,000 crores for the metro project. But you decided to do the opposite.'

'Let's not get into that discussion now. I don't have time. All I have is real estate. My money is all tied up in real estate, not so much in cash. I also have to pay salaries for this month –'

'Look Rana, we all know how difficult the market is these days. Since yesterday it has turned upside down. The chief minster would help if he were in a position to do so. But with elections round the corner, I don't think –'

'At least, can I meet the chief minster? I have invested in his son's news channel. Today it's worth thousands of crores. I invested in his campaign. He won the elections. I have been –'

'The CM can't talk now. There's a crisis meeting going on with the high command in Delhi.'

'Meeting with the high command? What? About me?'

'The chief minster is planning to build a five-star tourist destination on the hill site of Tirumala. If you have money to invest, you are welcome. Otherwise, it's useless to wait. You know how it is.'

'I have real estate I could offer as collateral. It's worth every rupee and more,' Rana pleaded. 'I need some backing now.'

'I'm sorry, Rana. Really, truly sorry, but there isn't anything we can do for you any more.'

Jagjivan was the first to look at Rana with pity in his eyes and he would not be the last.

Rana lowered his head and stared at the ground uncertainly.

TWENTY-TWO

22 July 2008

At 10.00 a.m. on 22 July 2008, Rana paced the length of his office, his hands clasped behind his back. Then he stood near the window for a while, quietly observing the security man with a gun guarding the premises ... He slowly walked back to his computer. A blank word processor stared back at him from the screen.

Rana was about to write an e-mail that would ruin his life forever. He had been, by nature, illogical. But today his decision to write an e-mail to the board members and stock exchange officials confessing his misjudgements was an attempt at playing the victim to generate sympathy. His motive was to salvage whatever little he could from the catastrophic losses incurred due to his premature decisions.

'Dear Board Members,' he began, 'it is with deep regret, and tremendous burden that I am writing this message –'

Rana went on to list his misjudgements, ranging from his investment in VEMAYHTAS to non-existent cash in

Sathyamev's account, all to save Sathyamev from sinking further or being taken over by the competitors. He went on to give other silly details that made for a good five-page, scandalous read.

'It was like riding a tiger,' Rana wrote in a poetic frenzy, 'without any hope of being rescued. I'll now subject myself to the law of the land.'

The only story he left out of his confession was his fear of getting mauled by the tiger called Kanu, his nephew.

At 10.45 a.m. that day, the chairman of SEBBI received an e-mail from Rana Rajput's official e-mail ID. After reading it, he couldn't believe his eyes. It had to be a fake. He immediately summoned his assistant to check the e-mail's authenticity.

At 10.50 a.m. the same day, a thin crowd gathered around Kiran Shah's desk at the *Afternoon Times* office. The moving graph on his monitor resembled the flight path of an airplane on a suicide mission. The green line of the flight path continued sliding unabated.

'The market is baked,' Mayank shouted.

'Bloody hell, Sathyamev is a fraud company. I always told you guys, the stock market is only for the scammers,' Suhail gleefully added.

At 11.00 a.m. the same day, a renowned news anchor reporting live from his studio couldn't catch his breath. The ever-smiling and eternally optimistic advisor on the channel had never imagined that a company the size of

Sathyamev would one day make news for all the wrong reasons. He looked like he had been punched in his belly and forced to report the story that very instant. 'We are too shocked to digest the news. Let me read out Rana's confession, again, so that we can make sense of it. The first big revelation from Rana's e-mail is that *Sathyamev's cash is gone*. The second big revelation is, and I quote, "Sathyamev's accounts are fictitious." And the third –'

By the time the anchor finished reporting the story, he almost looked constipated. 'I'll never in my life understand how any promoter could sink his own ship,' he signed off.

Almost at the same time, Arvind Kumar was in his element discussing the downfall of Sathyamev with his expert panel on NewsReview TV.

At 11.15 a.m. panic had gripped Dalal Street. *How could Rana ever do this to his own company? If the content of the e-mail is true, will this spell doom for Sathyamev's investors? What about thousands of employees – who will recruit those poor souls?* But the most important question everyone seemed to be asking was: *Why did Rana confess?*

Thousands of miles away in Singapore, Kanu was on the phone discussing his next clandestine mission. The clock showed 1.50 p.m.

'Yes, that's perfect. Sathyamev's stock will slide further. Wait for an hour or so till the stock dips below twenty.

Then it's all ours for the taking. Remember, twenty is the magic number. We go in, we buy as much as we can.' Kanu then paused to listen. 'Yeah, twenty because that's where my dad left this company. Yes, you are right. It's all happening now!'

Kanu smiled, then stood up from the comfort of his sofa and walked a little distance to turn off the television screaming news of Rana's confession.

'You're coming?' he asked.

Darshu looked confused. 'Where? And why did you turn it off? That's news about –'

'C'mon, that's news you already know.'

'C'mon don't be so arrogant!'

'You coming?'

'Where?'

'I want to send a photo of us to my mom.'

'How sweet! You didn't tell me about that – where are we going?'

'To a studio. Before that we have to go to a small temple that sells special items. We've to collect a few props from there.'

'Props?'

Inside the studio, Darshu was decorated with pearls and flowers and given an emerald-green lehenga choli to wear to go with her red dupatta. Kanu was dressed in a gold-embroidered red jacket, a light-blue dhoti and a golden kamarbandh. He sported a colourful garland around his neck, a flute in his hands and a peacock feather in his crown.

The couple posed for the camera, smiling, as the photographer said, 'Say cheese.'

The man fired the camera and an image of Radha-Krishna emerged from the instant photo camera: it was a sight to behold.

Kanu looked at the photo and turned to his companion. 'Didn't I tell you I am Kanha? Here's the proof!'

ACKNOWLEDGEMENTS

I am grateful to my brother, Shailesh Singh, and bhabi, Vasanthi Singh, for their constant assistance, encouragement and guidance, without which this book would not have been possible.

I must also thank my nephew, Parth Singh, my sister, Sareeta, and brother-in-law, Prakaash Singh, for their support.

I am lucky to have friends who stood by me in my hour of need. Sincere thanks to: Raju Parmar, Vinaynath N., Murali, Sanjay Kumar, Ravikanth M.R., Dilsad Gani, Janantik Shukla, Jose Kottanani, and many others. I am also thankful to Sudhir Chacha, Dr Nishindra Kinjalk and Navin Singh for their words of encouragement during my stay in Muzaffarpur.

Somak Ghoshal, Managing Editor at HarperCollins, edited the manuscript; I am grateful for his assistance.

I am indebted to Shivani Vellanki, Mrs Suman Malik and Dr R.K. Malik for reviewing the manuscript and providing invaluable feedback.

And finally, I owe my greatest debt to Mom and Dad for their blessings and encouragement.